THE RETURN OF
MR. CAMPION

ALSO BY MARGERY ALLINGHAM

Blackkerchief Dick
The White Cottage Mystery
The Crime at Black Dudley
Mystery Mile
Look to the Lady
Police at the Funeral
Sweet Danger
Death of a Ghost
Flowers for the Judge
The Case of the Late Pig
Dancers in Mourning
The Fashion in Shrouds
Black Plumes
Traitor's Purse
Dance of the Years
Coroner's Pidgin
More Work for the Undertaker
The Tiger in the Smoke
The Beckoning Lady
Hide My Eyes
The China Governess
The Mind Readers
Cargo of Eagles
The Darings of the Red Rose

NOVELLAS & SHORT STORIES

Mr. Campion: Criminologist
Mr. Campion and Others
Wanted: Someone Innocent
The Casebook of Mr Campion
Deadly Duo
No Love Lost
The Allingham Casebook
The Allingham Minibus
The Return of Mr. Campion
Room to Let: A Radio-Play
Campion at Christmas

NONFICTION

The Oaken Heart: The Story of an English Village at War

AS MAXWELL MARCH

Rogue's Holiday
The Man of Dangerous Secrets
The Devil and Her Son

THE RETURN OF MR. CAMPION

AN ALBERT CAMPION MYSTERY

MARGERY ALLINGHAM

OPEN ROAD
INTEGRATED MEDIA
NEW YORK

ISBN: 978-1-5040-9273-9

This edition published in 2024 by Open Road Integrated Media, Inc.
180 Maiden Lane
New York, NY 10038
www.openroadmedia.com

MYSTERY WRITER IN THE BOX
BY MARGERY ALLINGHAM

The art of writing mystery stories is much like any other art, one part aberration to three parts dedication, but when Kipling observed that there were nine and sixty ways of constructing a story he was not including the Mystery in the generalisation.

The Mystery is never included in literary lore: that is one of its peculiarities. Something like sixty percent of all books borrowed in many English public libraries are mystery stories and yet they are always reviewed by themselves, kept quite apart from orthodox fiction. This is not mere literary segregation, the black writing and the white writing kept asunder, but rather an indication that the Mystery is different, just as Astrological Prediction is different, or Letters to the Editor.

To my mind the one really extraordinary thing about it is that it is conventional to the point of being rigid, in an age when every other kind of writing tends to be without prescribed form. This is as odd, when one considers it, as if there were an enduring popular passion for the triolet in an era of free verse.

It is not that changes have never been attempted, but, although the pattern has softened, no radical alteration has yet occurred. The Mystery remains box-shaped, at once a prison and a refuge.

Its four walls are, roughly, a Killing, a Mystery, an Enquiry, and a Conclusion with an Element of Satisfaction in it.

To please the majority, each of these items must be balanced, at least factually convincing and, if possible, new. This is an exacting specification. Both writers and readers are relentlessly precise, and, when moralists cite the modern murder mystery as evidence of an unnatural love of violence in a decadent age, I wonder if it is nothing of the sort, but rather a sign of a popular instinct for order and form in a period of sudden and chaotic change. The essential killing is, at worst, no more than a status symbol, an indication that the theme in hand is of importance. But there is, also, something deeply healthy in the implication that to deprive a human being of his life is not only the most dreadful thing one can do to him but also that it matters to the rest of us.

The view of the Mystery as a refuge is particularly attractive to me because that is how I came into it.

I wrote my first some nine years after the end of the first world war. I was twenty-two at the time but already at the end of a long apprenticeship, and I was very nearly dead of premature old age and disillusionment. Perhaps I should explain. My difficulty had been that I was a writer by birth and that, alas, has nothing whatever to do with being a born writer.

When I first surfaced, about the age of six, I discovered myself to be the odd man out in a community which did nothing but sit in silence and write. We were a successful Edwardian family living on the edge of the Essex salt marshes, taking no notice of our neighbours, and keeping our own peculiar hours. My father had married his first cousin in his late thirties and had given up editing a London magazine to live in the country and devote himself to writing the rolling melodrama stories which filled the British equivalent of the American pulp magazines.

He wrote at least two five-thousand-word installments a week and sometimes a third in a lighter vein about boys at boarding school, and he worked hard and slowly, never for a moment relaxing the enormous care which ensured his success.

My mother was very much younger and was one of those remarkable women who can always succeed in the thing that everybody else is doing and with much less effort than they. She did not write for so long as the others, but she did do it and sold the products, reaping a sort of awed unpopularly in consequence. The other writers were visitors, friends of my father's from his days in Fleet Street. There was always someone extra closeted upstairs, working to a press date or finishing some long speculative task.

My clearest recollection is my own frustration. I was energetic, affectionate, and lonely, and all the interesting people in the world appeared to be on the other side of glass. There was nothing for it but to join the club, and soon, I too, sat alone with a stone bottle of blue-black ink and faced the first two great problems of my trade: *How to say What?* It was a hard life but I expected that. Everybody I knew remarked on it at some time or other.

One of my favourite brother brushes at this time was an elderly Irishman named George Richard Mant Hearne. He was a great friend of the family and often stayed with us. He was bald and surprised looking, with a stiff leg which gave him a great stride to his walk. He came from Cork and was witty and gentle and poetical and quite different from ourselves, who were second generation London Irish and packed with intellectual savagery and a curious delight in self-derision. Mr Hearne wrote fairy stores [sic] for fun and, for a living, a three thousand word weekly adventure concerning either Sexton Blake or Robin Hood. He worked with care and precision, his basket full of spoiled pages. I used to accompany him to the post office and, as he always enquired very politely after my work, I used to ask after his.

I learned of many of the hazards of my profession from his accounts of his crises. There was the time when the artist had a lost weekend and forgot which series he was illustrating. The first my poor friend heard of it was when it was discovered that the block, already made for the next week's Robin Hood, showed a company of persons sitting in the greenwood dressed in the flannels and boaters fashionable in the current year of nineteen hundred and ten.

Mr Hearne rose to the occasion with courage and inserted a single sentence in his tightly knit piece. '*Swiftly disguising themselves in modern costume, Robin Hood and his Merry Men took counsel.*' He was not pleased with it, though. It held up the action, he said, and then, like one of the witches in his own fairy stories, he gave me a riddle to remember. 'They never mind you putting all you've got into this sort of stuff. They never pay you any more for it, but they don't stop you.'

So ever since those days, I have always kept some item on the stocks which has got to be given all I have. There is nothing uplifting about this: I do it for pleasure. Sometimes it has to take its turn, but I never put it away.

By the time I was twenty, I had tasted some of the Dead Sea fruit of authorship. My left, or 'commercial', hand was reasonably successful. I earned an almost adequate living by writing and re-writing a great many words to suit the less important requirements of a variety of editors. But my right hand, the one I took so seriously and which wrote 'for fun', was not doing so well.

It had produced two full-length books, the first a novel about smuggling on the salt-marsh, which was the only place I knew well. Smuggle was all one could do there save graze.

This book had been published on both sides of the Atlantic when I was seventeen, and I had been to a full-scale London literary party on the strength of it. I had also had my first unnerving experience of being interviewed by the daily press without having anything to say to it.

My poor father was bitterly disappointed by the mess I made of it all. He was the kindest man alive, but, in one of his stories, I would have been beautiful as well as industrious, witty, resourceful, and, above all, lucky so that my book would have coincided with some world-wide interest in smuggling on salt-marshes. As it was, I had the family figure, designed by Providence for great endurance at the desk, no conversation and a stammer. My book sold few copies and irritated quite a lot of people.

My second was even more unfortunate inasmuch as it never got published at all. I wrote it at the direct request of my father who was one of those born editors who are able, not only to inspire almost anybody to write anything, but whose decisions are final anyhow. At this time, he was bitten with curiosity concerning one of the most controversial subjects of the day, degenerate teenagers or Bright Young People as they were called.

I did my honest best to produce the work he ordered: 'a factual truthful account of the Inmost Thoughts, Aspirations and Actions of the Young as You Know Them', and I achieved something so abysmally and innocently dull that it exhausted the reader very nearly as much as it had me. The book was a great disaster and I almost became entirely left-handed and gave up writing except for a living.

Only then did it occur to me that, as far as writing for fun was concerned, I might profitably dispense with absolute direction, and I recalled Mr Hearne's remark about the freedom to be found in the simple action story. The Mystery had begun to blossom, and the rules were very strict, but their restraint was negligible compared with the dreadful strait jacket of keeping bitterly serious when one was not that way inclined. I decided to escape into the Mystery.

At this distance it is much easier to see what I was running from than it was then.

In 1928, the postwar demolition of Edwardian civilisation was well under way. Few people had any faith in anything constructive and the mood was angry. Discredited ideas suffered in a general spring-cleaning so drastic as to be almost a laying waste.

Many perfectly good babies thrown out with the bath water and several eternals nearly went with them.

The chief of these last was Romance, even the word lost its normal meaning and became a synonym for a watered down version of the period's main discovery which was that sex could be discussed.

In the twenties, one could have fairly described the Mystery as 'that kind of popular tale which is not about the Horrors of Love'; and the odd effect of this arbitrary division was, that into it went every familiar demigod which the ordinary reader wanted to keep amid the jamboree of destruction.

One of the first of these ancient treasures was the knight errant. This figure is Romance's eternal hero, the rescuer, the dragon slayer, the wanderer in search of other people's troubles. When he became a displaced person he went into hiding and lived on, as Reggie Fortune, Philip Marlow, Philo Vance, and Perry Mason, as the Good Fairy Private Eye, in fact…an unlikely sprite.

However, likeness was by no means so important in the early days as it became later on. Realism, even the Mystery's brand which is literal, rather than lifelike, has seeped into the form very slowly. The knight errant flourished in his fancy dress, and the writers, who continued to develop him in his exile, were left in peace to do so. They were in the sanctuary of the four-sided box and were never taken too seriously either by themselves or anyone else.

From the author's point of view, one of the more deceptive aspects of the Mystery is that it appears so easy to do, and I suspect that I was particularly fortunate inasmuch as that was practically the only mistake I did not make. I had never found any writing easy and this was to be right hand stuff. What attracted me most of all, I remember, was the protective covering offered to the author. Nobody blamed the Mystery writer for being no better than himself. If he got his facts wrong the readers wrote and abused him, but no one, not even in the literary columns, ever wrote to analyse his twisted ego or to sneer at his unformed philosophy. Nobody cared what the Mystery writer *thought*, as long as he did his work and told his story. It suited me. The only definite thing I had to tell the world was that I liked it, even if no one else did. The box seemed most inviting, but settling down in it was a very tricky business. At that time, I had no idea of the importance to the writer of his knight errant detective. I thought that one simply had to have a sleuth who was instantly recognisable, so that the reader could follow him without effort...an opium smoker in a deer-stalker, perhaps. Most of the more showy types appeared to have been bagged by the time I came in, and, on looking around, my eye lighted on a minor character called Albert Campion in my own first detective story. True, he was not very suitable and, indeed, had been described in that book as some sort of minor crook, but I did not think anyone would ever read *Black Dudley* again, and so I promoted him.

He appealed to me because he was the private joke-figure of we smarter youngsters of that period. The Zany or Goon, laughing inanely at danger, who is now beloved and imitated by most young people everywhere was, in those days, considered a very unhealthy and esoteric phenomenon. He was misunderstood and regarded with black misgiving by all but the enlightened few and the idea of making him a detective in a lighthearted Mystery story was absurd and rather fun.

So there we were for a time, me and Albert. He was a piece of youthful nonsense and I was growing up; we seemed set for trouble.

For a while I was fully occupied finding out how to write the tales at all. From the start, my Mysteries have tended to run in threes, one to break the new ground, one to consolidate it, and one to convince me I must push on again. This has nearly always meant that the second book was the good one, and so, in later years, the third of the series has not always been written, even if it has been partially worked out.

The first three, *Black Dudley*, *Mystery Mile*, and *The Gyrth Chalice Mystery*, were constructed on the Plumpudding principle. One collected as many colourful, exciting, or ingenious inventions, jokes, incidents, or characters, as one could lay hands on and simply crammed them into the box as tightly as they would go. This is no construction at all, and I should never have got away with it had my left hand not been trained in the old school of 'pop' adventure which decrees simply: 'a surprise every tenth page and a shock every twentieth'. As it was, it made a definite recipe of a sort and I survived to go on to phase two. This was an attempt at the straight murder mystery, the tale cut to fit the box. *Police at the Funeral* was the first of these, and *Death of a Ghost* the second, and, before they could be written, something had to be done about Mr Campion.

Fortunately for me, it occurred to me then that if I could change so could he, and that the difference between a real character and a paper one was life which changes all the time. As the only life I had to give anybody was my own, we grew very close as time went on.

After the Murder Mysteries, we had a shot at the light novels and, after them, at a more serious kind, lightening the proceedings every now and again with a Plumpudding single to keep our amateur status. Since then, I have experimented steadily, developing, I suspect, rather like a painter, who grows tired of one technique quickly, and is always searching for a new one; but all my tales have been delivered to the reader packed in the Mystery box. Mr Campion has wandered through them all as, indeed, so have I. As far as I'm concerned, one is just about as real as the other.

This sidelight on the mechanism is only absolutely true of one Mystery writer, but, as I reflect on some of my contemporaries and their creations, I cannot think that I have been entirely alone in my approach. It seems to me that the peculiar way in which the *genre* has developed and become adult in the last thirty years suggests that quite a number of the writers, who have grown up with it, and have flowered despite the form, must have been refugees too, in a period of world emotional chaos. It is only since the 1914 war that the novelist has been considered, of necessity, an angry or cynical figure. Before then, many quite unindignant people were read and respected. The belief has been that the times have been so wry that a whole generation of writers has been soured by them, but my bet is that gay and grave people are born and not made. One either finds life entertaining or one does not, and what happens in one's life has amazingly little effect upon the basic outlook.

One interesting point is that much of all this must have been instinctively understood at the time. Extraordinary measures were taken to keep the Mystery to itself. For one brief era, there was a suggestion that it was not a story at all but a game, a sort of fox hunt with the author doubling and weaving and the readers after his blood.

Then there was the class question; interested people were always trying to raise our status by giving us little tips on English and inventing new rules and ethics. I remember swearing on a skull in front of Miss Dorothy Sayers, who was severe in pince-nez and Mandarin coat, that I would 'never cheat'. I had an over-developed sense of humour in those days but I swore most sincerely; it seemed important. G K Chesterton was there, but he laughed, I noticed.

At times it has been a chastening ride for any aspiring writer of Comedy. For a short while, Mysteries were published with their last two chapters sealed to prevent any March Hare reader from gulping them backwards and disappointing himself; and one year, there was an attempt to bring the tales out in mock type-script to look like police-case files, real clues (bits of hair, half matchsticks, or a thorn with a scrap of worsted on it) stuck about the pages in small Cellophane bags.

Mercifully this sort of thing proved unnecessary. The readers did not tire of the Mystery as the publishers had feared. They were in sanctuary too, all shut up together with their authors in the box ('ark' might perhaps be the better term), all getting by with their treasures in a time of danger.

The change in the emotional climate has come very slowly, and nowadays, young novelists, who are neither furious, nor even particularly depressed, need not hide anymore. The Mystery has remained, however, and growing skill has made its shape much more flexible, although the four walls remain. Today it has become the Folk Literature of the twentieth century and is, in a way, a modern version of the Morality plays of the Middle Ages. Historians tell us that the Moralities, those crude but popular pantomimes of personified Vice and Virtue which were performed upon open wagons in the market places, are only of interest since they served to link the Mystery and Miracle Plays, which were frankly religious, with the later secular Theatre. But I should have thought they might have had a humble little purpose of their own.

As does the modern Mystery, they stated an elementary theory of Right or Wrong, Growing or Dying, in a cheerful, popular way, to a generation of ordinary people who were exposed to a great new flood of contradictory beliefs, cynical theories and some of the most demoralising hazards civilised humanity has ever experienced. The Bomb is hard to live with; so, no doubt, was the Plague.

Nowadays, the Mystery goes everywhere. The same sagas appear, almost simultaneously, in every language, in every country. The same knight errants — disguised at the moment as regular police — comfort pillows as far apart as New York, Sydney, and Peru; as Berkeley Square, London, and a straw hut in a native village in Rhodesia. The main message is still the same, simple and on the side of the Angels: 'It is not good to die; any violent death is the concern of the Community'.

Minor messages vary as do the writers, and some of these may have been hampered by the formality of the medium, but, for the rest, and I count myself among these, the Mystery is an art form whose discipline has been beneficial and which has always kept us free in our very unimportance. We have the privilege of Court Fools. There is very little we dare not say in any company in any land. Nobody honours us more for blurting out the truth if it occurs to us; but then, as Mr Hearne said, nobody stops us.

THE CASE IS ALTERED

Mr Albert Campion sat in a first-class smoking-compartment reflecting sadly that an atmosphere of stultifying decency could make even of Christmas a stuffed-owl occasion. Suddenly a new hog skin suitcase of distinctive design hit him on the knees, the golf-bag brushed the shins of the shy young man opposite him and an armful of assorted magazines burst over the pretty girl in the far corner of the compartment. A blast of icy air swept round the carriage. The familiar jerky movements which indicated the train had started, a squawk from a receding porter, and then Lance Feering burst in propelled, as it seemed, by rocket.

"Caught it," said the newcomer with the air of one confidently expecting congratulations, and as the train took the points he teetered back on his heels and collapsed between the two young people on the seat opposite Mr Campion.

"My dear chap, so we notice," murmured Campion, and he smiled apologetically at the girl now disentangling herself from the shell-burst of newsprint. It was his own particular disarming my-poor-friend-is-afflicted variety of smile, the one that privately he considered infallible, but on this occasion, it let him down.

The girl, who was in her late teens, slim and fair, with eyes, as Lance Feering put it later, "like brandy-balls," looked at Campion with grave interest. She packed the magazines into a neat bundle and placed them on the opposite seat before returning to her book, and even Mr Feering, who was in one of his more exuberant moods, could not fail to notice that chilly protest. He began to apologise.

Mr Campion had known Feering in his student days, long before he became a well-known stage-designer, and was used to him, but now even Campion was impressed for Feering's apologies were easy but also abject. He collected his bag, stowed it in a clear space on the rack above the shy young man's head, thrust his golf clubs on the opposite rack and, positively blushing and regarding the girl with pathetic humility, he reclaimed his magazines.

When he spoke, the girl glanced at him, nodded coolly and with just enough graciousness not to be gauche, and then calmly turned over a page.

Mr Campion was amused. When at the top of his form Lance was reputed to be irresistible. His dark face with its long mournful nose and bright eyes was sufficiently unhandsome to be interesting and the quick gestures of his short, painter's hands made his conversation picturesque, but his singular lack of success on this occasion clearly astonished him and he sat back in his corner eyeing the young woman with covert mistrust.

Mr Campion resettled himself for the two hours' silence which custom demanded from first-class travellers who, even though in all probability are soon going to be asked to dance together if not to share a bathroom, have not yet been introduced.

There was no way of telling if the shy young man and the girl with the brandy-ball eyes knew each other, or if they too were *en route* for Underhill, Philip Cookham's Norfolk place. And for himself, Campion was inclined to regard the coming festivities with a degree of lugubrious curiosity. Cookham was a magnificent old boy, of course, "one of the more valuable pieces in the Cabinet," as someone had once said of him, but Florence was altogether a different kettle of fish. From wealth and position she had grown blasé to both and now took her delight in notabilities, in Campion's experience a dangerous affectation. She was, he had to admit it, some sort of remote aunt of his.

He looked again at the young people, caught the boy unaware, and was immediately interested.

The illustrated magazine which the lad had been reading had fallen to the floor and he was staring out of the window, his mouth drawn down at the corners, and a narrow frown between his thick eyebrows. His was not an unattractive face, too young for strong character, but open enough in the ordinary way, yet at that moment it wore a revealing expression. There was recklessness in the twist of the mouth and sullenness in the eyes. And the hand upon the inside armrest was clenched.

Mr Campion was curious. Young people do not usually go away for Christmas in this top-step-at-the-dentist frame of mind.

The girl looked up from her book. "How far is it to Underhill from the station?" she inquired of the young man.

"Five miles," he replied. "They'll meet us." He had turned to her so easily and with such obvious affection that any theories that Campion was forming about him were immediately knocked on the head. The man's troubles were palpably nothing to do with unrequited love.

Lance had raised his head with bright-eyed interest at the gratuitous information and now a faintly sardonic expression appeared on his lips. Campion sighed for him. Lance Feering fell in and out of love with the abandonment of a seal round a pool. He was an incurable optimist and already he was regarding the girl with that shy despair that so many women had found too piteous to be allowed to persist. Metaphorically Mr Campion washed his hands of Lance. He turned away just in time to notice a stranger glancing in at them from the corridor. It was a dark and arrogant young face and Campion recognised it immediately, feeling at the same time a deep wave of sympathy for old Cookham. Florence had done it again.

Victor Preen, son of old Preen of the Preen Aero Company, was certainly notable, not to say notorious. In his short life he had gathered to himself much publicity by his sensational flights, and a great deal more for adventures far less creditable, which drew from angry men in the armchairs of exclusive clubs many diatribes against the blackguardliness of the younger generation.

Victor Preen stood now a little to the left of the compartment window leaning idly against the wall, his chin up and his eyelids drooping. At first sight he did not appear to be interested in the occupants of the compartment, but when the shy young man looked up Campion caught a swift glance of recognition, and something else, passing between them.

Then, still with that same elaborate casualness, the man in the corridor wandered away, leaving the other staring in front of him, his eyes again sullen.

The incident passed so quickly that it was impossible to define the exact nature of that exchanged glance, and Mr Campion was never a man to go imagining things, which was why, when they arrived at Minstree Station, he was surprised to hear Henry Boule, Florence's private secretary, introducing the two men to each other, and even more surprised to notice that they met as strangers.

The rain cascaded as they came out of the station and Boule, who, like all Florence's secretaries, appeared to be suffering from an advanced case of nerves, bundled, as it seemed, all the passengers from the train into a shooting-brake, a small car and two Daimlers. Before they drove off Campion looked around with some dismay at Florence's Christmas bag. She had surpassed herself. There were more than half a dozen celebrities, a brace of political highlights, an angry-looking lady novelist, Nadja from the ballet, a startled academician and Victor Preen, and others who looked as if they might belong to art, sport, money, or might even be their relations.

Mr Campion had been separated from Lance and was looking for him when he saw him in one of the cars, with the novelist on one side and the girl with the brandy-ball eyes on the other. Victor Preen made up the ill-assorted four.

As Campion was an unassuming sort of person, he had been relegated to the brake with Boule himself, the shy young man and all the luggage.

Boule introduced them awkwardly and collapsed into a seat, wiping the beads from his forehead with relief that was a little too blatant to be tactful.

From the introduction Campion learnt that the shy young man's name was Peter Groome. Throughout the uncomfortable journey they talked in a desultory fashion and Mr Campion gathered that young Groome was in his father's firm of solicitors, that he was engaged to be married to the girl with the brandy-ball eyes, that her name was Patricia, and that he thought Christmas was a waste of time.

"I hate it," Peter said with a sudden passionate intensity which startled even his mild companion. "All this sentimental good-will-to-all-men business, it's false and sickening. There's no such thing as good will. The world's rotten."

No sooner had he spoken than he bit his lip and turned away to the streaming landscape. "I'm sorry," he murmured, "but all this bogus Dickensian stuff makes me writhe."

Mr Campion made no direct comment. Instead, with affable inconsequence, he murmured, "Was that young Victor Preen I saw in the other car?"

Peter Groome turned his head and regarded Campion with the steady stare of the wilfully obtuse. "I was introduced to someone with a name like that, I think," he said carefully. "He was a little baldish man, wasn't he?"

"No, that's Sir George." The secretary leaned across the

luggage to support him. "Preen is the tall young man, rather good-looking. He's *the* Preen, you know." He sighed. "Millionaires get younger every day, don't they?"

"Obscenely so," said Peter Groome abruptly, and returned to his despairing contemplation of the rain-washed landscape.

Underhill was *en fête* to receive them, and as soon as Campion observed the preparations his sympathy for young Groome increased, for to a jaundiced eye Florence's display might well have proved as dispiriting as Preen's bank balance. As she herself said in a loud voice, even while she linked her arm through Campion's, clutched the academician with a free hand and captured Lance with a bright bird-like eye, "we've gone all Dickens." The great Jacobean house was festooned with holly. An eighteen-foot tree stood in the hall. Yule logs blazed on iron dogs in the hearths and already the atmosphere was thick with that curious Christmas smell which is part cigar-smoke and part roasting food.

Philip Cookham stood receiving his guests with pathetic bewilderment. Every now and again his features broke into a smile as he greeted some face he knew. He was a distinguished-looking man with a fine head and eyes permanently worried by his country's troubles.

"My dear boy, delighted to see you. Delighted," he said, grasping Campion's hand. "I'm afraid you've been put over in the dower house. Did Florence tell you? She said you wouldn't mind, but I insisted that Feering went over with you, and also young Peter Groome." He sighed and brushed away Mr Campion's hasty reassurance. "I don't know why the dear girl never feels she has a party unless the house is so overcrowded that our best friends have to sleep in the annex," he said sadly.

The "dear girl," looking not more than fifty-five of her sixty years, was clinging to the arm of the lady novelist and the two women were emitting mirthless parrot-cries at each other. Cookham smiled.

"She's happy, you know," he said indulgently. "She enjoys this sort of thing. Unfortunately I have a certain amount of urgent work to do this weekend, but we'll get in a chat, Campion, some time over the holiday. I want to hear your news. You're a lucky fellow. You can tell your adventures."

Mr Campion made a face. "More secret sessions, sir?" he inquired.

The Cabinet Minister threw up his hands in a comic but expressive little gesture before he turned to greet the next guest.

As he dressed for dinner in his comfortable room in the small Georgian dower house across the park, Campion was inclined to congratulate himself on his quarters. Underhill itself was just a little too much of the ancient monument for strict comfort.

He had reached the tie stage when Lance appeared. He came in, very elegant indeed and highly pleased with himself. Campion diagnosed the symptoms immediately and remained deliberately and irritatingly incurious.

Lance sat down before the fire and stretched his sleek legs.

"It's not even as if I were a good-looking blighter, you know," he observed invitingly when the silence had become irksome to him. "In fact, Campion, when I consider myself, I simply can't understand it. Did I so much as speak to the girl?"

"I don't know," said Campion, concentrating on his tie. "Did you?"

"No." Lance's denial was passionate. "Not a word. That hard-faced female with the inky fingers and the walrus moustache was telling me her life story all the way here in the car. The dear little poppet with the eyes was nothing more than a warm bundle at my side. I give you my dying oath on that. And yet — well, it's extraordinary isn't it?"

Mr Campion did not turn round. He could see the artist quite well through the mirror in front of him. Lance had a sheet of notepaper in his hand and was regarding it with that mixture of feigned amusement and secret delight that was typical of his eternally youthful spirit.

"Extraordinary," he repeated, glancing at Campion's unresponsive back. "She does have nice eyes. Like licked brandy-balls."

"Exactly," agreed the lean man at the dressing table. "I thought she seemed much taken up with her fiancé, young Master Groome," he added tactlessly.

"Well, I noticed that, you know," Lance admitted, forgetting his professions of disinterest. "She hardly recognised my existence in the train. Still, there's absolutely no accounting for women. I've studied 'em all my life and never understood 'em yet. I mean to say, take this case. The girl ignored me, avoided me, looked through me. And yet, look at this. I found it in my room when I came up to change just now."

Mr Campion took the note with a certain amount of distaste. Lovely women were invariably stooping to folly, but even so he couldn't accustom himself to the spectacle.

The message was very brief. He read it at a glance and for the first time that day he was conscious of that old familiar flicker down the spine as his experienced nose smelt trouble. He re-read the four lines:

There is a sundial on a stone pavement just off the drive. We saw it from the car. I'll wait ten minutes there for you half an hour after the party breaks up tonight.

There was neither signature nor initial, and the summons broke off as baldly as it had begun.

"Amazing, isn't it?" Lance had the grace to look shame-faced.

"Astonishing," Campion's tone was flat. "Indeed, staggering old boy. Er — fishy."

"Fishy?"

"Yes, fishy, don't you think so?" Campion was turning over the single sheet thoughtfully and there was no amusement in the pale eyes behind his horn-rimmed spectacles. "How did it arrive? In a plain van?"

"In an unaddressed envelope. I don't suppose she caught my name. After all, there must be some people who don't know it yet." Now Lance was grinning impudently. "She's batty, of course. Not safe out and all the rest of it. But I like her eyes and she's very young."

Campion perched himself on the edge of the table. He was still very serious. "It's disturbing, isn't it?" he said. "Not good. Makes one wonder."

"Oh, I don't know." Lance retrieved his property and tucked it into his pocket. "She's young and foolish and it's Christmas."

Campion did not appear to have heard him. "I wonder," he said again. "I should keep the appointment, I think. It may be unwise to interfere, but yet I rather think I should."

"You're telling me." Lance was laughing. "I may be wrong, of course," he said defensively, "but I think that's a cry for help. The poor lass evidently saw that I looked a dependable sort of chap and — er — having her back against the wall for some reason or other she turned instinctively to the stranger with the kind face. Isn't that how you read it?"

"Since you press me, no. Not exactly," said Campion, and as they walked over to the house together he remained thoughtful and irritatingly uncommunicative.

That evening Florence Cookham excelled herself. She exhorted her guests "to be young again," with the inevitable result that long before midnight Underhill contained a company of ruffled and exhausted people.

It was one of Florence's more erroneous beliefs that she was a born organiser and that the secret for good entertaining was to give everyone something to do. Thus it was that Lance and the academician — now even more startled-looking than ever before — found themselves superintending the decoration of the great tree while the girl with the brandy-ball eyes acted as Mistress of Ceremonies for a small informal dance in the drawing room, while the lady novelist scowled over the bridge table and the ballerina steadily refused to organise amateur theatricals.

Only two of Florence's party remained exempt from her tyranny. One was Cookham himself; he looked in now and again, but whenever his wife pounced on him, he was ready with the excuse that he had more urgent work waiting for him in his study. The other was Campion; he had work to do on his own account and he had long-since mastered the difficult art of self-effacement. Experience had taught him that half the secret of this manoeuvre is to keep discreetly on the move; he strolled from one party to another, always ready to look as if he belonged should his hostess's eye come to rest on him inquiringly.

For once his task was comparatively simple. Florence was in her element. She rushed about surrounded by breathless assistants and at one time the very air in her vicinity was thick with coloured paper, yards of ribbon and a snowstorm of address tickets as she directed the packing of the presents for the school-children's tree, a second arboreal monster which stood in the ornamental barn beyond the kitchens.

Campion left Lance to his fate which promised to be, at the most modest estimate, three- or four-hours' hard labour and continued his purposeful meandering. His lean figure drifted among the company with an apparent aimlessness which was utterly deceptive. There was, in fact, hidden urgency in his lazy movements and the pale eyes behind his spectacles were alert and unhappy.

He found Patricia dancing with young Preen and paused to watch them. The man was in somewhat flamboyant mood, flashing his smile and his noisy witticisms about him, but the girl was far from content. As Campion caught sight of her pale face his eyebrows rose. For an instant he almost believed in Lance's unlikely suggestion. The girl really did look as if she had her back to the wall. She watched the doorway nervously, her shiny eyes full of fear.

Campion looked about him for the other young man, but Peter Groome was not in the room, nor in the hall, nor yet among the bridge tables, and even half an hour later he had not put in an appearance.

Campion was himself in the hall when he saw Patricia slip into the anteroom which led to Philip's private study, that holy of holies which even Florence treated with wholesome awe. Campion had paused to enjoy the spectacle of Lance, wild-eyed and tight-lipped, wrestling with the last of the blue glass balls on the guests' tree, when he saw Patricia disappearing round the familiar doorway under the branch of the double staircase.

It was what he had been waiting for and yet, when it came, his disappointment was unexpectedly acute. He liked her smile and her brandy-ball eyes. Patricia had left the door ajar and Mr Campion pushed it open an inch or so further, pausing on the threshold to consider the scene within. The girl was on her knees before a panelled door which led into the inner room and she was trying, somewhat ineffectively, to peer through the keyhole.

Campion stood looking at her regretfully and he did not move when she straightened and paused to listen, with every line of her young body taut with the effort of concentration.

Philip's voice amid the noisy chatter startled him and he swung round to see the minister talking to a group on the other side of the room. A moment later the girl brushed past him and hurried away.

Campion went quietly into the anteroom. The study door was still closed, and he moved over to the period fireplace beside it. This fireplace, with its carved and painted front, its wrought-iron dogs and deeply recessed inglenooks, was one of the showplaces of Underhill.

The fire had died down and the interior of the cavern was dark, warm and inviting. Campion stepped in and sat down on the oak settle, where the shadows swallowed him. He had no intention of being unduly officious, but his quick ears had caught

23

a faint sound from the study and Philip's private sanctum was no place for furtive movements when its master was out of the way.

Mr Campion did not have to wait long. The study door opened quietly, and someone came out. The newcomer moved across the room with a nervous, unsteady tread, and paused abruptly with his back to the quiet figure in the inglenook. Campion recognised Peter Groome and his thin mouth narrowed. The younger man stood irresolute, his hands behind him and one of them holding a flamboyant parcel wrapped in the coloured paper and scarlet ribbon that littered the house. A sound from the hall flustered him and he spun around and thrust the parcel into the inglenook, the first hiding place to present itself, and turned to face the new arrival.

It was Patricia. She came slowly across the room, her hands outstretched, and her face raised to Peter's.

Mr Campion thought it best to stay where he was, and indeed he had no time to do anything else for Patricia was speaking urgently, passionately.

"Peter, I've been looking for you. Darling, there's something I've got to say and if I'm making an idiotic mistake then you've got to forgive me. You wouldn't go and do anything silly, would you? Would you, Peter? Look at me!"

Peter had his arms round her, and his laugh was unsteady and not very convincing. "What on earth are you talking about?"

She drew back from him and peered earnestly into his face.

"You wouldn't, would you? Not even if it meant an awful lot. Not even if, for some reason or other, you felt you had to. Would you?"

He turned from her helplessly, great weariness in the lines of his sturdy back, but she drew him round, forcing him to face her.

"Would he what, my dear?"

Florence's arch inquiry from the doorway separated them so hurriedly that she laughed delightedly as she came briskly into the room, her hair-style a trifle dishevelled and her draperies flowing.

"Too divinely young. I love it!" Florence said devastatingly. "I must kiss you both. Christmas is the time for love and youth and all the other charming things, isn't it? That's why I adore it so. But, my dears, not here. Not in this silly, poky, little room. Come along and help me, both of you, and then you can slip away and dance together as much as you like, but don't come in this room. This is Philip's dull part of the house. Now, come along this minute. Have you seen the precious tree? Too incredibly distinguished, my darlings, with two great artists at work on it. You shall both tie on a candle. Come along!"

Like an avalanche she swept them away and no protest was possible. Peter shot a single horrified glance toward the fireplace, but Florence was gripping his arm; he was thrust out into the hall and the door closed firmly behind them.

Campion was left in his corner, and the parcel on the opposite bench not a dozen feet away. He moved over and picked it up. It was a long flat package wrapped in holly-printed tissue. It was unexpectedly heavy, and the ends were unbound.

Wrestling with a strong disinclination to interfere, Mr Campion turned it over once or twice but a vivid recollection of the girl with the brandy-ball eyes in the silver dress, her small pale face alive with anxiety, made up his mind for him. He sighed and pulled the ribbon.

The typewritten folder which fell onto his knees surprised him. It was not at all what he expected, and neither was its title, "Report on Messrs Anderson & Coleridge, Messrs Saunders, Duval & Berry and Messrs Birmingham & Rose," immediately enlightening, and when he opened it at random a column of incomprehensible figures confronted him.

It was a scribbled pencilled note in a precise hand at the bottom of one of the pages which gave him his first clue: "These figures are estimated by us to be a reliable forecast of this firm's full working capacity."

Mr Campion's face was grim.

Two hours later when Mr Campion picked his way cautiously along the clipped grass verge down to the sundial walk, it was bitterly cold in the garden and a thin white mist hung over the dark shrubbery which lined the drive. Behind him the gabled roofs of Underhill were shadowy against a frosty sky. There were still a few lights shining in the upper windows, but below stairs the entire place was in darkness.

Mr Campion huddled his greatcoat around him and plodded on, unwonted severity in the lines of his thin face. He came at last to the sundial walk and there he paused, straining his eyes to see through the mist. He could make out a figure standing by the stone column and heaved a sigh of relief as he recognised the jaunty shoulders of the Christmas tree decorator. Lance's incurable romanticism was going to be useful at last, he reflected with wry amusement.

Campion did not join his friend but instead withdrew into the shadows of a clump of rhododendrons where he composed himself to wait. He disliked the situation in which he found himself. Apart from the extreme physical discomfort involved he had a natural aversion toward the project in hand, but little fair-haired girls with shiny eyes can be very appealing and Mr Campion had once been a very young man himself.

It was a freezing vigil. He could hear Lance stamping in the mist, swearing softly to himself, but even that supremely comic phenomenon had its unsatisfactory side.

Campion was shivering, and the mist's damp fingers seemed to have stroked his very bones. Suddenly he stiffened. He had heard a rustle behind him and presently there was a movement among the wet leaves, followed by the sharp ring of feet on the stones. Lance swung round immediately, only to drop back in astonishment as a tall figure bore down upon him.

"Where is it?"

Neither the words nor the voice came as a complete surprise

to Campion, but the unfortunate Lance was taken entirely off his guard.

"Why, hello, Preen," he said involuntarily. "What the devil are you doing here?"

Preen stopped in his tracks, his face a white blur in the uncertain light. For a moment he stood perfectly still and then, turning on his heel, he made to take off without uttering a word.

"Ah, but I'm afraid it's not quite so simple as that, my dear chap." Campion stepped out of the shadows and, as Preen passed, slipped an arm through his and swung him round to face the startled Lance who was coming up at the double.

"You can't clear off like this," Campion continued, still in the same affable, conversational tone. "You have something to give Peter Groome, haven't you? Something he rather wants?"

"Who the hell are you?" As he spoke Preen jerked up his arm and might have wrenched himself free had it not been for Lance, who though completely in the dark had recognised Campion's voice and was quick enough to grasp certain essentials.

"That's right, Preen," he said, seizing the man's other arm in a bear's hug. "Hand it over. Don't be a fool. Come on, hand it over. Hand it over, my boy, don't be an idiot."

This double attack appeared to be inspirational. They felt the powerful young man stiffen between them and when he spoke his voice had a tremor in it.

"Look here, how many people know about this?"

"The world..." Lance was beginning cheerfully when Campion forestalled him.

"We three and Peter Groome," he said quietly. "At the moment Philip Cookham has no idea that Messrs Preen's curiosity concerning the probable placing of government orders for aircraft parts has overstepped the bounds of common sense. You're acting alone, I suppose?"

The question went straight to the mark.

"Oh, lord, yes, of course." Preen was cracking. "If my old man gets to hear of this I — oh, well…"

"I thought so." Campion sounded content. "Your father has a reputation to consider. So has our young friend Groome. You'd better hand it over."

"What?" There was a note of slyness in Preen's question and Campion laughed contemptuously.

"Since you force me to be crude, whatever it was you were attempting to use as blackmail, my precious young friend. In fact, whatever it may be that you hold over young Groome and were trying to use in an attempt to force him to let you have a look at a confidential government report concerning the orders which certain aircraft firms are likely to receive in the next six months. In your position you could have made pretty good use of information like that, couldn't you? But what you could have over Groome, I haven't the faintest idea. When I was young it might have been objectionable companions, but that's no longer the fashion, is it? What's the modern equivalent? An RD check?"

Preen said nothing. He put his hand into an inner pocket and drew out an envelope which he handed to Campion without a word. Mr Campion examined the slip of pink paper by the light of the pencil torch and when he spoke his tone was not pleasant.

"You kept it for quite a time before trying to cash in on it, didn't you?" he said. "Dear me, that's rather an old trick and it was never admirable. Young men who are careless with their bank accounts have been caught out like that before now. It simply wouldn't have looked good to Peter's legal-minded father, I take it? You two seem to be hampered by your respective papas' integrity. Yes, well, you can go now."

Preen hesitated, opened his mouth to protest, but thought better of it. Lance looked after his retreating figure and then turned his attention to his friend; his eyes were bright and inquiring in the half-light.

"But who wrote that note?" he demanded.

"Victor Preen, of course," said Campion brutally. "He wanted to see the report, but he was making absolutely sure that it was young Groome who took all the risks of being found with it. With Preen's special knowledge he only had to glance at the file to get all the information he needed to pick up quite a packet."

"Victor Preen wrote the note," Lance repeated blankly.

"Well, naturally," said Campion absently. "That was obvious as soon as I saw the file. He was the only man in the place with the necessary knowledge to make use of it. That's what bothered me in the beginning. I couldn't see what on earth we were in for."

Lance made no comment. He pulled his coat collar more closely about his throat and stuffed his hands into his pockets. Campion was tactfully silent.

But the artist was not quite satisfied for later that evening when Campion was sitting in his dressing gown writing a note at one of the small escritoires which Florence had so thoughtfully provided in her guest bedrooms, he came in again.

"Why?" he demanded. "Why me? Why did I get the invitation?"

"Oh, that was just a question of luggage." Campion spoke over his shoulder. "That bothered me at first, I admit, but as soon as we fixed it on to Preen that little mystery became blindingly clear. Do you remember falling into the carriage this afternoon? Where did you put your elegant piece of gent's natty suitcasing? Over young Groome's head. Preen saw it from the corridor and assumed the chap was sitting under his own bag. He had the note delivered to the room of the owner of the new pigskin suitcase. That's how it was, I'll bet on it."

Lance nodded regretfully. "Very likely," he said sadly. "Funny thing. I was sure it was the girl."

Lance came over to the desk. Campion put down his pen and indicated the written sheet.

Dear Groome [it ran],
  I enclose a little matter that I should burn forthwith, if I were you.

The package that you left in the inglenook is still there, right at the back on the left-hand side, cunningly concealed under a pile of logs. It has not been seen by anyone who could possibly understand its contents. If you were to nip over very early this morning you could return it to its properly appointed place without any trouble. If I may venture a word of advice, it is never worth it.

The author grimaced as he re-read his own words. "It's a bit avuncular," he admitted, "but what else can I do? His light is still on, poor chap. I thought I'd stick it under his door and wash my hands of the entire affair."

Lance chuckled. He was grinning. "That's fine," he murmured. "Old Mr Campion does his stuff for reckless youth. All we need now is the signature and that ought to be obvious as everything else has been to you, damn you. I'll write it for you. 'Merry Christmas. Love from Santa Claus.'"

"Your point," said Mr Campion. "Game, set, and match."

MY FRIEND MR CAMPION

From my point of view one of the oddest things about my friend Mr Campion is that here we are in 1935, I've known him for eight years and I haven't the faintest idea who he is or what sort of yarn I shall be called upon to retail about him next. I know his name is assumed and, of course, from time to time I have been able to pick up odd pieces of information he has let fall in the course of the various of his adventures I have chronicled, but who he is and what his real name is I am not merely not at liberty to divulge: I simply do not know.

We met first, as later I found out, in what was a highly characteristic fashion. Early in 1927 I was writing *The Crime at Black Dudley*, a book about an exciting and mysterious affair taking place in a strange, gaunt old house. I was a quarter of the way through the book and the perfectly good hero was behaving very well indeed in the most trying circumstances. There was a dinner party and I was peacefully describing it when I noticed that there was one character too many — or rather that there was a stranger in the little party I had so carefully assembled.

I don't want it to be thought that I am one of those dear old ladies who just write down the first thing that comes into their heads and hope the finished page will be entertaining. Rather I am one of those pernickety souls who plan and re-plan, who build up and weed out and scrape and niggle away in their minds until they know just exactly what sort of story they are going to write, who the characters are and all about them.

Moreover, I have very strong views on the subject. I believe that an author who cannot control his characters is, like a mother who cannot control her children, not really fit to look after them. So this stranger at the Black Dudley dinner table startled me and made me feel terribly uncomfortable.

Campion butted into the conversation, I remember, with a most unsuitable remark, in tone much too flippant for the grim proceedings, and I became aware of him as vividly as if I had turned my head and suddenly seen him.

At first sight he was not exactly prepossessing, but lately he has looked much better, but then he's getting on, all of thirty-five, and age is hardening him a bit.

In 1927 he was just as I then described him: a tall, pale young man with sleek yellow hair, enormous horn-rimmed spectacles and an abysmally foolish expression. As is everyone else who does not know him, I was fooled by that expression and I had no idea of the hidden shrewdness, the quick, practiced brain or the lovable disposition concealed beneath that negligible exterior.

I tried to turn him out of my story; I did not think his line in imbecile chatter an adornment to my sober tale, but all my efforts to shake him off were of no avail. As soon as I got going on a conversation between two characters out leapt an absurd remark and the pale young man was there again.

Dismayed, I gave up work for a week and thought I had lost him but as soon as I returned to the Black Dudley dinner party there he was, smiling inanely and chattering away like a cross-talk comedian.

In the end I gave up the struggle and after that he took over possession. The hero, a plumpish young barrister, muffed his high spots and Campion popped up at the last moment and saved the situation very neatly.

In spite of myself I began to like him, he was so resourceful, so courageous and always a perfect little gentleman, but I could not get used to his wisecracks or his habit of saying the silliest thing at the most awkward moment.

That Black Dudley business was certainly his affair, but I was not happy about him. He seemed to be on some very shady business, for two or three embarrassing moments I thought he was a crook and, because in the penultimate chapter of my book he faded out of the story as suddenly as he had come into it, I never found out quite what his status was.

I met him next when I was writing *Mystery Mile* and when (in the first chapter) I found him on board the SS *Elephantine* I was pleased to see that he looked a little less effete.

Of course, I had planned a story with him in mind but in *Mystery Mile*, as afterward in every Campion story, I did not actually plan his part. From the very beginning he always saw to that himself and now I have come to rely on him in the same way that one relies upon an old and trusted collaborator.

It was in *Mystery Mile* that we really got to know each other. Early on he handed out his visiting card:

MR ALBERT CAMPION

Coups neatly executed
Nothing sordid, vulgar or plebeian
Deserving cases preferred
Police no object

PUFFIN'S CLUB
THE JUNIOR GREYS

and in the course of the story I saw for the first time the inside of his flat over the Police Station in Bottle Street and met for the first time Magersfontein Lugg, his "gentleman's man," as he called him.

I have always liked Lugg. Though by that time I had reached the stage when I took everything Campion told me with a grain of salt, I believed him when he said that Lugg had been a burglar and that he was "a very useful chap". He certainly was extremely useful in the later stages of *Mystery Mile* and it was then that his huge, white, miserable face became as familiar to me as Campion's own.

It was down at Mystery Mile that I met Biddy Paget. Campion met her there too and it was all rather uncomfortable for a while because I was rather fond of Campion and, though I could understand Biddy preferring the American, young Marlowe Lobbett, I did not like to see my hero slighted.

However, although I never thought him quite so light-hearted again, when next we met — and he handling a very delicate little job for the Treasury — he seemed perfectly happy.

That story was called by us *Look to the Lady* and by the Americans *The Gyrth Chalice Mystery*, and when it was done, I thought I knew all there was to know about Campion except his name, but he had a surprise for me. Until I wrote *Police at the Funeral*, I had never seen him handling a murder mystery and I had meant to leave it all to Inspector Stanislaus Oates of Scotland Yard, but Campion turned up again in the first chapter, and I must say he astonished me. He subdued his natural exuberance to the gravity of the circumstances and fitted into that grief-stricken, terror-ridden Cambridge household without giving offence to anybody. Moreover, he was decidedly helpful, quite as much so, in fact, as he had been in the hand-to-hand fights in *Mystery Mile* and *Look to the Lady*. Frankly, I was delighted to discover that he had a brain capable of genuine observation and deduction as well as his natural ability to wriggle out of a tight corner or worst a dangerous enemy.

As usual, he got on well with all the other characters — from my point of view not the least of his charms — he even endeared himself to Great Aunt Caroline and he certainly saved Uncle William from arrest.

After that, when we were truly old friends, I chronicled his adventures in the Pontisbright heirloom case (which we called *Sweet Danger* and the Americans, for some reason, *Kingdom of Death*). Amanda Fitton turned up during that business and I thought he was going to fall for her and get tied for life to the little baggage, but perhaps the memory of Biddy still rankled; anyway, he escaped to go to the assistance of sweet old Mrs Lafcadio in *Death of a Ghost* (a title which, if you only think of it, gives away the whole mystery). In that, to date the most ambitious of his efforts, he distinguished himself.

His latest experience — he certainly leads an adventurous life — is in another murder case. Campion thinks my account should be called *Flowers for the Judge* and from that title anyone familiar with English legal custom will guess what he has let me in for.

This is about all I can tell you about Albert Campion. I like him, and I like to consider myself his best friend but, even so, to me he is still a mystery. I know he was born on May 20th, 1900. I suspect he was at Rugby — he has just a touch of the Rugby manner. He says he went to St Ignatius College, Cambridge, and I know that he embarked on his exciting career in 1924. I know that he belongs to Puffin's Club and to the Junior Greys and that his address is 17a Bottle Street, Piccadilly, London W1, but who his people are, what his name is and what he does on his holidays, so to speak, alas, I cannot tell you.

However, he is sometimes indiscreet. Sometimes he lets his tongue run away with him. So — you never know. I live in hope.

THE DOG DAY

There is a time-honoured theory that the mysterious, the uncanny, the miraculous, and even the plain honest-to-goodness peculiar are properly appreciated only in a half-light.

Mr Albert Campion sat on a rock in the blaze of a pure white dawn, reflected on this notion, and rejected it. He rubbed his eyes cautiously with his bathing towel, but the old man, the girl and the dog did not disappear. They remained in earnest consultation just below him on the dazzling sand.

They had not seen him, and, because it is natural to prefer not to intrude oneself upon any sort of visual phenomenon, he remained perfectly still, his lean body melting into the pinkish crag behind him.

In all directions there was loneliness, not a sail or a ripple on the glassy water, not a parasol or a beach-pyjama on the sand, and in the near distance the planes and pinnacles of the discreet esplanade were as deserted as an empty plate.

The man and the dog sat facing one another and the girl looked down at them. They were all creatures of that slight fantasy which is the most fantastic of all: the not *quite* right. The girl was perhaps the most nearly normal, although sheer female beauty of such an idealistic kind is still sufficiently unusual to be surprising. As she stood, her weight on one hip and the dawn light turning her hair to white fire, she was quite sufficiently miraculous to take any ordinary man's breath away. The man and the dog were more unlikely. They were both so astonishingly formal. The man sat on a flat stone in much the same attitude and costume in which he might have presided at a board meeting. He was a smooth elderly person, meticulously shaved and dressed in pearl-gray suiting, white shirt and spats. A ring glistened on his little finger and an eyeglass dangled from his neck. The dog sat on the sand and he sat as anyone else might sit, with his legs stretched out in front of him, his only courtesy to dog construction the solid four-inch tail supporting much of his weight like the flap at the back of a photograph frame. He was smooth-haired and chocolate-coloured, with the lines and contours of a miniature carthorse, and he sat and surveyed the sea behind his friend with the thoughtful, contemplative air of one who rests.

Far up over the cliffs behind Mr Campion a cock crowed, and the girl straightened.

"It's getting late," she said unreasonably.

"Yes," said the man regretfully. "How do you feel about it, Theobald?"

The dog turned his head slowly, as though loth to take his eyes from the shining water. He sighed, an exaggerated gesture, and got up with dignity. He stretched carefully, each leg separately as dogs do, and then, before Mr Campion's startled eyes, went through a further process of limbering up, which dogs as a rule do not. He raised his left paw and let it dangle alarmingly, as though the bone were actually broken, repeated the exercise with his right, limply dragged his left back leg behind him and then did the same thing with his right back leg. He hung his head until his nose was buried in the sand, rolled over on his side with his eyes turned up, and finally, having satisfied himself that every single part of him was in reliable working order, set off at a portly stroll scarcely faster than his companions, who walked after him.

They passed out of sight, not with any haste nor yet with the dilatory luxury of those who stroll. They went purposefully, all three of them, as if such a promenade were essential to their career.

Having watched them go, Mr Campion went back to his hotel feeling a little lightheaded and uncomfortable. The tall houses of the seaside resort had still the blank eyes of sleepers and he felt like a trespasser in a dormitory.

As people sometimes do who get up very early in the morning because they cannot sleep, Mr Campion slept most of the day and when, round about cocktail-time, he descended into the lounge the light over the sea was the familiar blue and gold, the esplanade was dotted with parasols and the sands were alive with children of all ages and their coloured toys. The magical quality of the dawn had vanished, and the world was once more a solid material place of ice cream vendors, evening papers and white-coated waiters carrying drinks on trays.

Mr Campion remembered the vision of the morning with self-tolerant amusement and decided that the girl could not have been so beautiful, the old man so formal, nor the dog so — well — so business-like.

This was his first real introduction to the hotel, for he had arrived very late on the evening before and, as he sat in a corner sipping his sherry, a misgiving nudged him. The wine was good, and the room was charming, but he began to regret the well-meaning friend who had recommended the place as the ideal retreat for three days' complete rest. The hotel was exactly as the friend had described it, exclusive, quiet and thoroughly English, with good food and superlative service, but Mr Campion had forgotten that the natural corollary to these attributes is, of course, the next best thing to the silence of the tomb.

Everybody was there, all the dear old familiar faces; the

Colonel and his lady drinking in whispers in a corner, the elderly lady and her companion knitting with muted needles, the pleasant, plump Mama with the pretty twin daughters who looked away regretfully when the Colonel's young son glowered at them. The Anglo-Indian widow was there, alone and languishing over an iced drink and a magazine, the two bachelors who did not know each other but who sat close together for protection, the hearty young woman and her girlfriend who lowered their happy healthy voices the moment they laid aside their golf clubs in the hall and came to join the father of one of them dozing under a palm; these and several others, all exclusive, English and utterly quiet.

Mr Campion was not himself a jolly person but a long association with all sorts of people in the course of his profession, criminal investigation, had cured him of his native self-consciousness, and it rubbed raw his nerves to be in the presence of so many people who all clearly liked each other or at least considered so scrupulously each other's feelings that they were prepared to become virtually dumb lest they offend or discommode any of their own kind. It seemed to him that there must be among people who had in common this one great quality of self-sacrificial politeness other less spartan grounds for compatibility. Yet he knew, as who does not, that one unguarded remark addressed to a stranger must produce that swift change of colour, that guilty glance round, and that frigid commonplace which would but add another layer to the ice.

It was while he was wondering if a great national disaster would break the barriers, or if a natural phenomenon — pink snow, perhaps — would shatter this stultifying delicacy, that the chocolate dog came limping into the lounge. He was in a most pathetic condition. His left forepaw hanging helplessly, he dragged himself across the parquet on three faltering legs. Arrived in the centre of the room he collapsed with a thud and turned up his eyes.

Immediately there was a general rustle and a scraping of chairs and then the silence became absolute. The dog looked round him mutely, made a gallant attempt to sit up and beg, collapsed again and, just once, howled, very softly.

"Poor chap, he's hurt." It was one of the golfing young women. But before her solid brogues could carry her across the floor the Colonel had thrown down his paper, the elderly lady had cast aside her knitting and the two bachelors had risen to their feet. The Anglo-Indian woman was the nearest and was the first to the dog.

Five minutes later Mr Campion himself joined the anxious throng. The dog was a little better. A committee of experts had examined his foot. The Colonel gave it on his word that no bone was broken. The father of the golfing girl, who, it transpired, owned a pack of hounds, suspected rheumatism and the Anglo-Indian widow was inclined to agree with him. The plump Mama had persuaded the invalid to take a lump of sugar and the elder of the bachelors was holding the basin for her.

"A nice chap," said the Colonel's son to one of the pretty twins. "What is he?"

"Spaniel and Labrador, first cross," submitted the younger bachelor.

"Terrier somewhere there," said the Colonel.

"Hound, I should say, sir," ventured the elderly lady, "no doubt about it with those ears."

"A coloured gentleman anyway," giggled the prettier twin. "What's his name?"

They tried them all and the dog was helpful. At "Jack" he looked blank, at "Jim" bewildered. "Rover" seemed to amuse him, "Smith" left him cold, but at "Henry" he barked.

"That's the name of a friend of his," said the Colonel. "Seen a dog do that before."

"Rumpelstiltskin?" suggested the elderly lady's companion and all present thought what a very nice woman she was.

Mr Campion forgot his superiority complex. He cheated.

"Theobald?" he suggested.

The dog sat up and stared at him in astonished contempt. Never in all Mr Campion's career had he been faced with a glance of such withering disgust. A nark! The unspoken insult went home and Mr Campion blushed.

"He doesn't like that, does he?" said the Colonel, laughing. "What is your name, boy? Rex?"

The abashed Mr Campion turned away from the crowd and came face to face with the girl of the morning. She really was beautiful, he was surprised to see, as beautiful as she had appeared to be that morning. She was looking at him reproachfully, a faintly puzzled expression in her eyes.

"I'm sorry," he murmured.

"So you ought to be," she answered back and pushed through the crowd.

It took Mr Campion all the evening to get her to himself for the little hotel was now like a parrot-house. Since everybody knew everybody else it was only the late arrivals who were not talking. The Colonel, the elderly lady, her companion and the elder bachelor played bridge in an alcove; the plump Mama and the Colonel's wife chatted happily about their children; the widow listened to the father of the golfing girls; those young women joined the twins, the spare bachelor, the Colonel's son and a group of other young people.

Mr Campion found the beautiful girl in the hall waiting for the lift. "You're not going up already?" he protested. "It's livening up now. Won't you join us all?"

She shook her head. "It's not in the contract."

Mr Campion felt helpless. "I'm so sorry about the name," he began, "but you see, I saw you on the sands this morning with Theobald and your…?"

"Father," she supplied.

"With your father," he repeated. "I still don't understand, you know."

The girl laughed. "Don't you? I thought you were a detective."

"So I am," he said desperately, for the lift was descending. "That's one of the reasons for my disgusting curiosity. Look here, will you promise to give me an explanation tomorrow?"

"Tomorrow we shall be gone," she said and, stepping back into the lift, was whirled up out of his sight.

But the following morning, when he was lying awake wrestling with a distinct sense of frustration and regret, he was roused by a discreet tapping low down on his door.

Theobald was in the corridor, fit and hearty, with no trace of paw trouble. He cocked an eye at Campion, gave his tail a perfunctory wag, and dropped a small white slip at his feet before galloping off to the staircase.

Mr Campion took up the pasteboard and found it to be a professional card neatly engraved.

"Theobald and Co," it ran. "Introductions effected. Hotel-service a specialty."

On the back, there had been pencilled in round 1930 hand-writing, a single line.

"Primbeach next week."

THE WIND GLASS

After the Japanese man had spoken, the Chigwells' warm sitting room was painfully silent for a moment. The three other people present stared at their visitor with embarrassment.

Edward Chigwell sat very still, his loose, heavy mouth partially open and his bright blue eyes bent almost wonderingly on the yellow face smiling at him across the room. His wife, a large, placid woman with a loose, white skin, smiled at her husband half-apologetically, half-contemptuously. Their daughter, Aieda, sat between her father and the man. She, too, was startled and her smile was false.

Mr Tio Yasen smiled at them, then a slightly puzzled expression spread across his face and he began to speak again in his soft, almost inflectionless voice. "I am afraid I speak at the wrong time," he said. "The customs of our countries are so different. You will forgive me that I am so — so—" he paused for a moment seeking for the word and finally came out with "unpleasant." "I repeat — I ask you for your daughter for my wife." He stopped talking but continued to beam at them.

Slowly Mr Chigwell recovered from his surprise and as he did so, a dull red flush crept from under his collar and crept over his face until even his eyes seemed darker. "You want to marry my daughter?" he said loudly, thrusting his hand forward so quickly that the white tip of his cigar fell off on to his thick blunt fingers.

Mrs Chigwell made a little fluttering gesture toward him, but Mr Yasen saw nothing of this; it was with difficulty that he understood the language, but his host's direct question put him more at ease. He smiled again. "Yes," he said.

Carefully Mr Chigwell flicked the ash off his hand and his long mouth turned down shark-fashion into a dubious smile.

Mr Yasen waited politely. He was considering the result of his decision to take an English wife. He realised the seriousness of the step and the prejudice of his own people, but he had made up his mind and his offer was unhesitant. He glanced at Aieda. The girl sat stiffly toying with her cigarette.

Leaning back in his chair and surrounding himself with blue, sweet-smelling smoke, Mr Chigwell spoke again. "So you want my daughter, Mr Yasen," he repeated, his deep loud voice echoing coldly round the room. "You've not asked Aieda, I suppose?"

"Of course he hasn't." Aieda spat out the words irritably. "You know I wouldn't want to marry him."

The change in the Japanese man was almost imperceptible, but a change there was. His smile died, his dark eyes in their narrow sockets almost disappeared under the wrinkled lids, and his thin mobile lips set hard.

"Well, then," continued Mr Chigwell complacently, "if Aieda doesn't want you, there's no more to be said."

The man quivered and there was on his wooden face something that was almost surprise. Then his eyelids dropped even lower and he rose to his feet. "I regret," he said simply, and, standing by his chair, he made three formal little bows.

Mr Chigwell nodded graciously. Aieda stared angrily, and Mrs Chigwell smiled at Mr Yasen as she would smile at an acquaintance whose name she had forgotten.

Mr Yasen turned and walked quickly out of the room, his

shining shoes making no sound on the polished floor. A moment later they heard the front door shut.

Mr Chigwell laughed. "Damned cheek," he said.

In the long neat road outside, Mr Yasen turned and stared back at the lighted window. For a moment he stood quite still in the shadow. He was no longer the polite and impenetrable Japanese man, placid and diffident. All this was gone. Tio Yasen had been insulted by a man for whom he had nothing but contempt and by a girl he had wanted and for whom he would have risked the anger of his parents. The faint light of the stars fell upon his upturned face, then Tio Yasen began to laugh softly, and, turning quickly away, he went down the road toward the station.

For two months Aieda heard no more of him, but one stifling hot evening a letter and a parcel were delivered to the shrub-encircled villa in the long, orderly road.

Her curiosity aroused, Aieda took them and tore open the envelope. She read through the note and then handed it to her father with a self-conscious laugh and turned her attention to the parcel.

Mr Chigwell looked at the note and raised his eyebrows. A slight smile spread over his heavy red face, then he laughed. "The little man again, eh? I thought we had seen the last of him."

"Oh, but we have, Dad," said Aieda, "read what he says. He's going back to Japan and this—" she touched the parcel, "is his farewell gift. Poor fellow, I'm afraid I treated him very badly, but how could I help it?" As she spoke, she wrestled with the knot of silk cord which bound the package.

The stifling heat which all the day had hung over London seemed to Aieda to become more oppressive. The sky was dark and there was no breath of wind in the garden.

Suddenly the girl shuddered.

Her father looked up. "What's the matter?" he asked. "Cold?"

Aieda smiled. "No," she said, "I don't know why I shivered. Have you got a knife?"

The two younger children, Benjamin and Victoria, arrived to see what was happening. With sharp jerks of his knife Mr Chigwell cut the cord in two or three places, and Aieda, taking the package from him, pushed back the outer paper. Immediately a faint smell of flowers arose from the bundle, and they all sniffed appreciatively.

Within the brown outer covering there was a quantity of soft tissue paper printed with quaint oriental pictures and within this something wrapped in a wide embroidered handkerchief.

Mr Chigwell was amused. "Good Lord!" he said. "Get on with it. What next?"

Aieda stripped off the handkerchief and held out a long, lacquered box, exquisitely designed and painted. She opened it carefully. Inside was yet another parcel wrapped in a finer and more delicately embroidered handkerchief. The girl laughed. "Wow!" she said. "Can't you see him wrapping it up?"

She unfolded the handkerchief, disclosing yet another box. Mr Chigwell's amusement increased. "A long farewell, eh, what?" he said.

Aieda lifted the two carved wood fastenings and the lid fell off into her lap. Mr Chigwell and the children leaned forward involuntarily.

"Whatever is it?" said Benjamin putting up his hand toward the box.

Aieda jerked the box away from him. "Don't touch," she said sharply and added as she pulled out a jumble of painted glass and string, "Look — a wind glass."

There was no stir in the air of the garden and the little wafers of painted glass made no movement but hung silently from the brass ring held between Aieda's thumb and forefinger.

"Wind glass? What's that for?" Mr Chigwell raised his eyebrows as he examined the ornament.

"Oh, haven't you seen one? They're too trendy." Aieda laughed. "You see, you hang it up in an open window or somewhere, and when the wind blows it plays — see!" She shook the ring slightly and the wind glass tingled.

Victoria clapped her hands. "Pretty," she said. Benjamin nodded. Mr Chigwell sniffed and lit a cigar. "Oh!" he said. "I see, very charming."

There was an underlying note of disappointment in his voice which Aieda was quick to recognise. "The poor fellow must have been hard up," she said. "Look, it's chipped here and there, and this ring is positively worn thin."

"Eh?" Mr Chigwell looked at the ring with new interest. Then he held out his hand. "Let's have a look," he said. He examined it carefully for a minute or two. Then he glanced up. "This is a real antique, I shouldn't be surprised," he said, "it's hand painted, anyway."

Aieda rose and looked over his shoulder. "Do you see how each bit of glass has some characters on it between the flowers?"

Mr Chigwell took one of the crystals in his hand and looked at it. "Yes," he said. "I see — what do they mean, Aieda? You're the expert."

The girl shook her head. "I don't know," she said. "I can't recognise even one of them. It's very old, I should think."

"Old, eh?" Mr Chigwell's tone was satisfied again. "Oh, well, we'll hang it up," he said to Benjamin. "Go and get a hammer and a nail, Vicky."

In a moment the child was back, and her father mounted a chair and drove the nail into the soft woodwork of the veranda just opposite to the open French windows. The wind glass was then hung on the nail and Mr Chigwell climbed down to survey his handiwork.

The curiously shaped crystals hung perfectly quiet in the calm air. Shining and beautiful, but silent, as though waiting for something.

Mr Chigwell looked up at the lowering sky. "We shall have a storm tonight," he said. "A good job, too. This heat is stifling."

Aieda sighed and stretched her arms above her head. "Yes," she said, "all this thunder in the air gives me a headache."

Victoria laughed and pirouetted round the lawn. "Oh, I don't feel like that," she said. "I feel excited. I hope we shall have a storm."

Gathering up the remnants of Mr Yasen's packages, Aieda passed under the wind glass and the faint draft she made stirred the slender glasses. She stopped and turned back. "Did anyone call?" she asked.

Mr Chigwell looked up. "No," he answered. "I didn't hear anything."

The girl laughed. "Funny," she said. "I thought I heard someone say, 'Aieda.'"

Mr Chigwell shook his head. "No," he repeated, "I heard nothing."

His daughter seemed but half-convinced. "I was dreaming, I suppose," she said and ran into the house. As she did so, however, she passed to the right of the wind glass and this time there was no movement among the little painted crystals.

For another half-hour Mr Chigwell sat out waiting for the storm to break, but there was no change in the heavy, clouded sky and the atmosphere seemed to become even more oppressive. It grew darker and still there was no breeze anywhere. He pulled out his watch — a quarter to seven. Slowly he pushed back his chair and rose heavily to his feet. Then he turned and went into the house. As he did so, he knocked his head against the wind glass and jerked it half off its nail. He swore at it and pushed it safely on again. "Someone'll have that down if we're not careful," said Mr Chigwell.

Suddenly, far off down at the end of the long neat road, the leaves of a tall poplar tree began to tremble, and a little breath of cool wind fled over first one garden wall and then another until at last it ruffled the leaves of the sycamore tree at the end of the Chigwells' grass path and, flying swiftly over the laurel bushes and the tall sunflowers, crept round the corner of the veranda and swept through the wind glass softly, caressingly.

The children playing on a swing in the big laurel clump at the end of the lawn stopped so as to listen. In her room upstairs, Aieda leaned out of the window to hear the better.

The breeze was followed by another and the wind glass continued to play fitfully. It was uncanny music, sweet and yet frightening; now dying away completely and then bursting out into a positive jangle as a rougher wind chased its brother. Sometimes it was like water falling on to stones, sometimes like a tiny bell rung in the night; now and again it seemed almost to cry her name — "Ai-e-da!"; once or twice it had a strange sound, something that was almost a summons.

Aieda thought it rather attractive but Mrs Chigwell, sitting at the open French windows, braced her shoulders and said to her husband, "I don't like it. It gives me a most extraordinary feeling — listen!" She put up a plump white hand. "Doesn't that sound queer to you?"

Mr Chigwell listened. "No," he said in his deep matter of fact voice. "What do you mean — queer?"

His wife seemed confused. "I suppose I'm stupid," she said, "but to me it has an almost evil sound — there!" She broke off suddenly, a note of triumph in her voice. "Didn't you hear it then? A lot of queer little notes together like — like calls?"

"Calls?" Mr Chigwell looked mystified.

"Yes, as though it was calling something — something evil."

Mr Chigwell laughed. "Here, you want your dinner," he said, putting his hand on her arm. "Don't you get talking like that or we'll begin to wonder how many drinks you've had."

He got up and looked out into the fast-darkening garden.

All the while the wind glass played fitfully, tinkling loudly. The wind was getting up, the clouds were gathering fast and the suppressed excitement that belongs to the few moments of quiet before a storm quivered on every leaf in the garden.

Mr Chigwell turned round to look at his wife. "I told the children they could stay up a bit tonight, Flo," he said.

Mrs Chigwell nodded resignedly. "Very well, dear," she said, "but they ought not to be out as late as this. Where are they — in the laurels?"

Her husband stepped out of the French windows. "I think so," he said over his shoulder. "I'll go and fetch them."

The wind still hovered about the garden and the sky was very dark but as yet there was no rain. Mr Chigwell stalked across the lawn, the red tip of his cigar showing brightly in the half-light, and behind him the wind glass tinkled and chattered like a live thing.

As he neared the first clump of bushes, he took the cigar out of his mouth ready to speak, and, pulling aside one of the projecting branches, he put his head into the opening and peered into the centre of the clump.

"Kids…" he began, and then stopped suddenly, the words dead on his lips and his prominent blue eyes bulging still farther out of their sockets.

On the bare earth underneath the laurel bush there was a little crouching bundle. It was fairly dark and Mr Chigwell, after his first shock, thought the thing was a dog, and, as he did not approve of strange dogs in his laurel bushes, he put out a foot to kick it. As he did so the creature stirred. It lifted up its head and Mr Chigwell stared down into a small and evil face. It grinned up at him, the brown lips rolled back disclosing sharp teeth, and the eye sockets partly open showed black glittering eyes within. This in itself was terrifying enough, but, to Mr Chigwell's horrified eyes, the thing, whatever it was, seemed to be so unnaturally small, as small as a baby.

As he stared at it, the wicked grin on the terrible little face broadened and the creature began to laugh — a queer tinkling laughter uncomfortably like little bits of glass grating lightly together.

Mr Chigwell could hardly breathe, his blood seemed to rush up in his throat and choke him, a cloud passed before his eyes, and when he again saw clearly the bare earth under the laurel bush was empty. He fancied he saw two or three little shadows flickering through the shrubberies at the other end of the lawn.

He let the branch he was holding swing back with a jerk and a rustle of leaves and, straightening himself with an effort, he turned and walked back across the lawn with quick, irregular steps. A good half of his cigar still hung from his right hand. Absently he put it to his mouth only to throw it down almost immediately.

The wind blew gustily over the garden, twisting the tree tops to strange fleeting groups of statuary and there were rustlings and faint laughter all round the flower beds and in the dark crevices beneath the shrubs; while, above the whisperings, the wind glass tinkled and rippled and called, a positive sound among so much indefinite noise.

Mr Chigwell turned. "Victoria! Benjamin!" he called; his voice sounded jerky and nervous even to himself.

There was no answer, but he thought he heard whispers from behind the summer house. He called again. "Victoria! Vic-tor-ia! Benjamin! At once!"

There was the sound of movement just behind him and the children came out together, not from the summer house, but from a clump of bay trees and privet on the other side of the lawn. They were holding hands, laughing, and murmuring to each other, as though they shared some wonderful secret.

As soon as they came within earshot they stopped talking and approached him with such an air of assumed innocence that had he been himself at that moment Mr Chigwell would certainly have cross-examined them. As it was, he simply ordered them to bed.

"Oh, I say, Dad, you promised," Benjamin began at once.

"You promised," wailed Victoria.

Mr Chigwell looked down at them. "Go — go to bed," he said unsteadily.

"Dad, need we? Need we? Please, please, it's so important tonight — just tonight — need we?" Benjamin's tone was eloquent.

Mr Chigwell said nothing, he just glared at the children. There was a long pause. Then, "Go to bed — at once," said Mr Chigwell for the last time.

Victoria caught her brother's hand and pulled him away. As they went round to the back of the house, she whispered something to him, and they laughed. Then they turned to look back at the laurels, laughed again, and hurried out of sight.

Mr Chigwell walked slowly into the house and collapsed heavily in a chair. His mouth sagged, and he sat silent, staring in front of him. Of course, he had seen nothing. He was quite sure of that now. What could he have seen? It was absurd! Some trick of the light and shadow had deceived him. He sat up and smiled reassuringly to himself. Presently he lit another cigar. It was odd that one could be so easily startled, he reflected.

Aieda was curled up on the sofa. She held her mother's large Persian cat in her arms and was trying to soothe it.

"Poor pussy — po-oo-or pussy," she said. "Look, Dad, he's terrified of something. I can't quiet him. I suppose the heat has got on his nerves. As soon as he came in here, he went all dithery — didn't you, darling? Didn't you?"

Mr Chigwell looked round the room. Aieda jarred on him. "Where's your mother?" he asked.

The girl did not look up from the frightened animal who was clawing her dress and trembling.

"She went upstairs," she said lightly. "Felt a bit faint or something."

Mr Chigwell rose a little unsteadily. "I'll go up to her," he said, and, stifling an extraordinary impulse to run, he walked deliberately from the room.

Aieda sat alone for several minutes, nursing the cat. She could hear the wind rustling in the garden and the wind glass tinkling.

After a while she began to listen more attentively to the wind glass. It seemed to grow louder and louder. A breath of cold air blew through the room; she shivered, and the cat, who had been lying almost peacefully in her lap, now sprang on to the floor and stood facing the open window, its fur on end, its tail erect, its back arched and its eyes blazing.

Aieda looked from the quivering animal to the window and, for the first time in her life, she felt a slight sensation of fear. She sat stiffly on the sofa. The song of the wind glass beat into her brain so that it seemed as if she could think of nothing else, and then a slight sound outside made her start, her blue eyes fixed on the open doorway.

The cat jumped back on all four feet and began to spit and swear.

Then, just below the door handle, very silently and very slowly, there appeared a little mask-like face.

Aieda turned cold and her scalp seemed to contract.

The face came round the side of the door; a small gnarled body followed, and in another moment a grotesque and awful little figure stood peering in upon her from the dark veranda.

Like some fantastic carving it stood there grinning up at her, its body crooked and bent beneath a brightly-coloured robe. And the wrinkled face was grotesque and twisted as it sneered and laughed at her across the room.

The cat stood stiff with terror. Aieda was too frightened to move or speak.

Slowly the thing raised an ivory claw from beneath its gaudy sleeve and beckoned to her.

Fascinated, Aieda watched the long, crooked finger. It seemed to draw her toward it. Slowly and against her will she slid off the couch.

The little thing's grin grew wider and, with its twisted finger, again it beckoned. She tried to scream, but no sound would come. In spite of herself, she made a step toward the open window.

Outside, the wind glass tinkled and jangled with the sound of the laughter of a thousand devils. The terrible creature in the doorway continued to smile and to beckon.

Aieda stood swaying in the centre of the room. The thing glided back a little, motioning her to follow. She felt her foot move forward, the electric light seemed to flicker and dance. Aieda shut her eyes — still she was drawn forward — and now she felt the cold air on her face; in another moment she would reach the window.

"Have you seen Benjamin and...? Oh, whatever is the matter? Are you ill?" Mrs Chigwell paused in the doorway.

Aieda pulled up short. She felt dazed and giddy but the horrible fascination that had been drawing her toward the window was broken and the little genie had vanished. There was a sudden lull in the wind and the tinkling glass on the veranda was silent. Aieda turned to her mother, her eyes still wide and terrified. "What were you saying when you came in?" she demanded quickly.

"I was asking if you'd seen the children. They're not in their beds."

Another gust of wind swept across the garden and there was the sound of tinkling laughter from the porch.

Aieda started. For a second, she stood staring at the open window, where the wind rustled, swaying the heavy velvet curtains as it passed. Then she turned and, rushing past her mother, called to her father.

"Dad — Dad — quick — the children must be in the garden — quick!"

Mr Chigwell came running, his heavy face the colour of red sandstone, his blue eyes darkened, and his mouth hanging open. He rushed straight through the room and out into the wind-swept dancing garden. Mrs Chigwell followed him. Aieda got as far as the threshold and paused. In the whirling darkness without she could make out the forms of her parents as they ran across the lawn.

The bushes and trees seemed mad with excitement, they swayed and danced and chattered like wild things, and all the while the wind glass played, jangling, laughing, calling triumphantly.

Aieda peered into the darkness, fearing to move. She fancied she could see little distorted figures — hundreds of them — moving in the lower branches of the trees. Then she heard her father calling "Vic-tor-ia — Ben-jamin — Benjamin — Victoria — Victoria!"

The vagrant wind carried his voice in little fitful gusts of sound. Aieda strained her ears but there was no answering cry to her father's calls. Then, as she stood listening, Victoria's gurgling, joyous laugh rang out from behind the summer house. Next, she heard Benjamin's voice speaking to his sister, but it was so far off that she could not make out his words.

The wind glass jingled furiously, and a wave of rushing air swept over the garden. Somewhere a door clattered and banged. Again Victoria's laugh came to the waiting girl at the French windows but this time it was much farther off — somewhere beyond the sycamore tree.

Aieda shouted, straining to make her voice heard above the noise: "Vic, Vic, come back. Victoria, Victoria!"

There was a momentary lull in the wind, and she fancied she heard whispering among the bushes; then, very far off and high up, as though among the tumbling clouds, she heard the child cry again. This time it was a wail of terror. It came again, fainter and fainter still.

Aieda gasped and her eyes dilated.

"Victoria!" she screamed, throwing up her arms instinctively, "Victoria!"

Again a faint, frightened cry came back to her out of the darkness. Aieda hesitated, then she sprang forward, and, leaving the sanctuary of the lighted room, Aieda dashed out on to the veranda and the whirling garden beyond.

As she passed under the wind glass the cat darted between her legs. To avoid the animal, she sprang into the air, knocking her head into the dancing glass ornament.

The thin brass ring at the top was lifted off its nail and the wind glass crashed down around her face and on to the ground. Instantly, and almost as though the sound of breaking glass had been a signal, the wind dropped and the first few heavy drops of rain fell upon the grass.

Aieda paused. The excitement and horror that were in the garden a moment before had gone. The trees and bushes had their accustomed shapes and there were no new and frightening shadows. Straining her eyes she peered anxiously around her. She felt ashamed of her own excitement.

A moment later she heard Victoria's voice from somewhere down the end of the grass path. Then she could hear her father scolding the children for disobeying him. His voice was quite natural, she noticed. Another minute and they all came up. The children were subdued, and Mrs Chigwell was wiping her eyes, her husband was talking volubly, his face redder than ever.

They went into the house together. Benjamin and Victoria were sent to bed and Aieda and her mother and father stood for a moment. Although she could not understand what it was, Aieda felt that something extraordinary had just happened. It was as though she had been awakened from an unpleasant dream which she could but half-remember.

She frowned wonderingly, trying to understand, then she shrugged and smiled. After all, what did it matter?

"What have you done to your forehead, dear?" said Mrs Chigwell.

Aieda turned to the mirror above the mantelpiece. Then she took her handkerchief and wiped her forehead.

"Blood!" she said uncomprehendingly. "I suppose that beastly thing cut me when I knocked it down."

Mrs Chigwell looked at her daughter, and there was in her large pale eyes a look more intelligent than usual. "They say," she said, or so it seemed to the others, rather fatuously, "that once blood is drawn honour is satisfied."

THE BEAUTY KING

In the days when Ricci Blomme was the one competent
assistant in Picquet's hairdressing shop in Bray Street, Islington, the Process Blomme was a subject for ridicule, opprobrium
and, on occasions, for abuse.

Papa Picquet, himself a sad little man with the eyes of a
Madonna and the moustaches of a Victorian villain, used to
regard Ricci's florid exuberance with regret.

"He is a fool," he would say, peering at his client in the mirror,
"the man is mad. He stamps upon his bread and butter. It is
pathetic."

Ricci remained unsuppressed. The germ of greatness was in
him, and he recognised and fostered it. His quarry was beauty in
the female. He strove for it as men strive for power, he starved
himself to buy its chemical ingredients, he believed in it as in a
holy vision, and in the end, he created it and did not recognise his
masterpiece when he saw it.

At the time of his employment in Picquet's salon, which was
homely and a little dirty, he strode among the shiny plastic
curtains of the cubicles a Napoleon unrecognised. His great chest
strained against the bone buttons of his soiled white coat and his

61

wild black hair was ever in need of his professional attention. He was not a visual advertisement for Picquet, but his work was good, and he remained on sufferance. His conceit exasperated both Picquet and most of the customers. Like all true artists he was tactless.

"If you were only beautiful, madam," he would murmur in a moment of confidence to the volatile proprietress of The Lion next door as he superintended the delicate tinting of her hair, "then you would be happy. You would have lovers. Your wildest midnight dream would be realised...is it not so? Wait, wait until the Process Blomme is complete..."

It made trouble. Not unnaturally there were frequent altercations at the back of the shop. Both Blomme and Picquet shared an inability to speak any one language with ease. Accidents of birth and an aptitude for mimicry had deprived either of a specified tongue but they each expressed themselves with some fluency in a mixture of French, Italian and English, adding a Latin wealth of imagery to a Saxon crudity in the statement of fact.

Picquet insulted the process and Ricci insulted two generations of Mesdames Picquet.

During this period there were only two people in the world who believed in the Process Blomme. The first was Ricci himself, who spent his evenings at chemistry classes and his nights in research, and the second was Francine.

Francine was seventeen and not beautiful.

Her duties in the Picquet establishment were at once undefined and unending. They included the washing of the floor of the salon each morning before the shop opened and the scouring of the shampoo vases in the evening after it closed.

Francine and Ricci slept at the same lodging house in Old Compton Street, a circumstance which Madame Picquet considered of great significance. However, even her long Normandy nose could detect no irregularity in their relationship and

Madame Sousa, the concierge of the lodging house, was of a respectability recognised throughout Soho.

She was an Arlésienne and since Francine was also of that city it seemed only natural that she should give the girl a bed in the room behind the stove and a *"p'tit p'tit déjeuner"* in return for her services during those hours when she was not at Picquet's.

This arrangement suited Francine very well. She saw a great deal of Ricci. She was a small person, undersized and almost emaciated, with a sallow skin, a wide mouth inclined to droop at the corners, and two dark smudges of eyes set far apart beneath heavy brows.

Ricci never looked at her. He was aware of her and frequently honoured her with news of the Process, but his fine dark eyes never rested upon her face for two moments together.

Francine did not resent this. She was content to wait. For her Ricci was both the means and the end, both the giver and the gift. Her plan was elementary, and she contemplated it with the patient faith with which a votaress contemplates the celestial gardens.

When Ricci should achieve the Process Blomme and plain women should be plain no more, Francine, so her plan had it, would be his first client. In her rare moments of relaxation she would imagine herself slowly emerging from the plasters, a vaguely defined but eminently lovely being, exquisite and desirable.

Ricci would then look upon her. His bright brown eyes would quicken, and he would stretch out his hands.

Francine's dreams took her no further but swooned away deliciously, leaving her eager to struggle with the washing-up of Madame Sousa and the shampoo vases of Monsieur Picquet. Her life was simplicity itself.

Meanwhile things did not go smoothly. On the day of the great row when Picquet blew himself up to fighting size and fourteen bottles of assorted unguents were smashed upon the white wall at the far end of the Salon, Ricci and Francine left Bray Street, Islington, forever.

Ricci strode along breathless and exalted, his old overcoat buttoned over his white jacket and his face burning with righteous anger.

Francine trotted a pace or so behind him clutching a paper carrier containing his tongs, his scissors and his comb besides her apron.

Madame Picquet's Parthian observations tingled in her ears.

"If he were your lover one could have understood. When he is not even aware of you such fidelity is a degradation."

The crisp French phrases stung her, but she bore them resolutely. She had hitched her wagon to a star and travelling was bound to be uncomfortable.

Ricci was voluble. That *cochon!* That excrement! That ageing pervert! That Picquet! On the day on which the Process Blomme revealed itself to an enchanted world, Picquet should see himself in all the naked horror of the blessed truth and would vomit.

In silence, Francine agreed.

The next few months presented certain difficulties. The cost of the chemical ingredients of the Process were not negligible and the saveable margin of Ricci's income had never been wide. Francine took the place of Madame Sousa's maid of all work, Eva, who had, by the divine instigation of a providence working directly toward the fulfilment of the Process, chosen this particular period to become *enceinte* by a chef sufficiently affluent to support her.

Ricci filled his bedroom with paraphernalia and devoted himself to the fulfilment of his destiny, but it took time and there were disappointments.

Francine, staggering up the rickety stairs with a broom or clean linen, would find her Napoleon sleeping exhausted among his little jars or sitting sullen and unapproachable in a dirty shirt, his eyes fixed grimly upon the crazy roofs of the houses over the way.

Madame Sousa who was, she hoped, a woman of business was at first suspicious and then alarmed. So Francine worked harder. And because she was invaluable, and Madame was not committed to provide Ricci with board as well as bed, the account of Monsieur Blomme was allowed to run on.

Francine suffered agonies of delightful pain in these secret sacrifices for the Process and for its creator. These were sweets for which she was duly punished in the best providential manner by the outcome of the sacrifices themselves. Because she was so unbelievably overworked, because her presence in Madame's insufferable kitchen was a necessity which ensured the fruition of the Process, it came out that when Ricci began to need a model upon whom to experiment it was Madame's pallid twenty-year-old daughter Odette who was the obvious recipient of the honour.

Francine steeled her heart. It is necessary to suffer to be beautiful and to love is to endure.

The day on which Ricci actually succeeded in turning Odette into something on which the average passer-by would look with interest was not marked by any natural phenomena. Madame herself doubtingly consented to a complimentary trial of the Process Blomme and was volubly amazed and delighted by the result.

Francine, toiling in the basement, was summoned to see the miracle. She stood trembling in the doorway of Ricci's bedroom like the heroine in a nightmare pantomime where the ugly sisters were not ugly, and Cinderella was.

If the transformed Madame and Mademoiselle Sousa were not actually academically beautiful, at least they were very much more than personable. The Process Blomme consisted largely of a method by which the under-skin was rendered instantly mature when the surface peel was removed. It also included Ricci's private eyebrow treatment, his lip stain and his coiffure.

The change in both mother and daughter was startling. Ricci was in tears. He glanced at Francine in speechless ecstasy and waved his hand toward Madame.

Francine did not move or speak. Her eyes grew darker and her body sagged. It was a moment of intense emotion.

Ricci controlled himself. He threw out his arms. His great chest swelled and strained against the buttons of his shirt.

"I have Her!" he said. "I have Her fast! I have caught Her and put Her in a pot."

There is nothing so wearying as the ever-receding dream. Francine wept every night for a fortnight but not with ecstasy.

Her disaster was certainly not due to any conscious cruelty of Ricci's; she realised that. It was fate. Fate had made her unavailable at the moment when Beauty and the love which she confidently believed must instantly be attendant upon it might have been hers. Fate had decided that she must wait.

Meanwhile Ricci's affairs had begun to move. Madame Sousa was a woman of influence and her support had been magnificently purchased. Interviews were arranged, conferences took place.

Ricci still talked to Francine when she cleaned his rooms and she found her little wagon bumping along behind a star which threatened to shoot away into spheres beyond her comprehension.

If the Process Blomme had not been the Process Blomme but some lesser discovery doomed to shine and disappear, Ricci might well have been accused of losing his head, but since it was no less than what it was, it remains on record that he seized his opportunities, fired his backers with his own enthusiasm and soared happily upward toward those heights which he afterward achieved.

To say mat Graustadt made Blomme is to say that the jar makes the marmalade or the dust-jacket the book, but in the beginning, he was very useful. He was a small fair man, delicate in dress as in physique, and he came to Ricci from the original backer who was no fool. Ricci found the new shop off Regent Street embarrassingly clean and austere, but he recognised its advantages. The grey paint, pale gold carpets and cut-glass accoutrements made him feel lonely and inferior at first, but he stomached them because Graustadt had won his confidence.

Very wisely Monsieur Blomme remained in the background except when the actual operation was in process. Graustadt engaged the assistants, all of them people of education and sound hospital training, the backer arranged for the patents, and Ricci, with unexpected business foresight, saw that he was not cheated.

There was quite a contretemps about Francine. Both she and Ricci had taken it for granted that a place would be found for her in the shop, and when Madame Sousa and Graustadt both put up separate opposition Ricci was first amazed, then indignant and finally triumphant.

"She is a good girl, a hard worker. I like her," he said to Graustadt when he had won his point.

Graustadt shrugged his shoulders and smiled with an inference which was at once conciliatory and insulting.

Ricci saw the smile but because Francine was an unrecognised influence in his life, he did not understand it in the least. Not wishing to display ignorance he did not pursue the matter.

Francine took up a position at Chez Blomme as lowly as her situation at Picquet's, and Ricci's rise to fame and fortune was a period of bewilderment and the destruction of faith for her.

She saw him very seldom in these days. He receded from her. When she caught sight of his plump, white-coated figure hurrying through a crowd of respectful assistants, each one her superior, he was as far away as if she had seen him through a telescope.

Chez Blomme, which began as a moderately busy beauty shop, became a fortress besieged. The cocktail bars spoke of the Process in the hushed accents of the recently converted. Lonely women in big deserted houses, ageing women in youthful circles, women in love and women soured, joined the ordinary horde of beauty hounds who descended upon the small grey shop like a plague of starlings.

Legends began to spring up around Ricci as legends sprang up around Merlin. Ricci had magnetic hands. Ricci studied in Vienna. Ricci had secret ingredients flown from China.

The stories grew wilder as his fame increased and the evidence of the power of the Process became more widely distributed.

Graustadt took the situation in hand. From her lowly position Francine observed a change of policy. Chez Blomme became exclusive and exorbitant. It moved to a quiet Georgian house off Bond Street, whose elegant front door was not disfigured even by so much as a brass name-plate. Within it was cool, aristocratic and alarming.

Francine always used the basement entrance and, in these days, saw no more of Ricci, not even from a distance. Patrons so exalted that their names were not divulged to the assistants who attended the maestro came in their great cars, and after-hours certain ladies were treated secretly and for enormous sums.

Ricci grew sleeker and at night went home, to a mysterious flat which Graustadt had acquired for him, in a shining, chauffeur-driven car of his own. The chauffeur often had to wait in the basement for his overworked employer and he struck up a friend-ship with Francine. She did not speak very much but always evinced great interest when the man talked, and from him she learnt that "the boss" was a funny cove, that he never spoke of anything but his work or went anywhere save to his business.

This intelligence comforted Francine. At least her Napoleon was still a Napoleon on the march.

As the money piled up and the backer became positively respectful Ricci might easily have succumbed to the flesh-pots, but since his genius was of the true fire, he remained absorbed by the Process itself.

It was on a midsummer afternoon when even the cool rooms

of Chez Blomme smelt faintly of exhaust from the hot roadway that the momentous "disagreement" took place. Not only the news but the actual vulgar sounds of it penetrated throughout the whole house.

The effect was sensational. Epithet after epithet, roar after roar filtered through the fine old panelling, shaking the candelabra and shattering the rarefied atmosphere like a rowdy in a concert hall.

The old house, barely inured to the desecration of trade, winced beneath this final indignity and seemed to huddle the shreds of its Georgian elegance about it. Startled minions paused in their ministrations, incredulity in their eyes. Dignified but sophisticated clients pretended not to have heard, and in the basement, Francine listened, new hope in her heart.

Graustadt left. He fled. His pattering feet scuttled on the thick stair-carpet and were heard no more.

Ricci remained in his office, the door locked. When his secretary tapped furtively at a quarter to six, he answered her ungraciously and would not come out.

The staff went home at a little past the normal hour, an unusually silent crowd. Ricci's car stood in the street outside.

Francine remained alone in the basement. She was cleaning a tray of silver ash bowls and cigarette boxes when Ricci came in. He looked tired and dishevelled and was in stockinged feet.

He did not greet her but began to talk at once as though there had been no break in their regular communication.

"He thinks I am to be arranged," he said, his brown eyes blinking in his honest indignation. "I 'ave told 'im. I am Ricci Blomme. The Process is mine. The whole thing is 'ere in my head. I 'ave told 'im. 'Go to hell!' I said. 'Go to hell where you belong, you piece of pink effeminacy.' We shan't see 'im again. That's a good thing, eh?"

He sat down on the table and began to turn over the bits of silver with a plump thumb and forefinger.

"Muck," he said presently. "Don't waste your time with it. I don' want this sort of thing. What do they think I am? A pansy flower? I am Ricci Blomme, Francine. You know that, don't you? You know who I am. I don't want this sort of thing."

He threw out his hands with a gesture which included the house and its accoutrements and, pursing up his lips, made an expressive and derisive sound.

Francine was breathless. Her dark eyes were hidden, and a faint colour pierced the sallowness of her cheeks.

Ricci padded round the room, prying into cupboards. From time to time he emitted little disconsolate sounds. Finally he returned to his seat on the table.

"Look, Francine," he said persuasively as he held out his podgy hands, "look, these are the hands of Ricci Blomme. They can make any woman beautiful, any woman in the world."

The girl in the grey uniform raised her face and looked at him. Her eyes were secretive, and her lips parted. Hungry children look so.

Ricci was still explaining his point.

"Why should I hide myself, Francine? Why should I attend only to the few? It is not the ingredients of my Process that are so expensive. I tell you, Francine, I am a Napoleon, a Hercules…and they would turn me into a smart servant. 'Thith ith the way to make money'…" he imitated Graustadt's gentle lisp. "Francine, have I ever cared about money? Did I care for money at Picquet's? At Madame Sousa's? Never in my life. I don' care about money!"

"What are you going to do?" Francine's voice trembled a little.

Ricci laughed. It was the fat mischievous chuckle of a child.

"I'll show you. I am going to manage my own publicity. I am going to show these fellers. I am the Beauty King! I am Ricci Blomme! You wait, Francine."

Francine smiled unexpectedly.

"Yes, I'll wait all right," she murmured.

Ricci eyed her suspiciously. "You stick around here all the same," he advised. "You'll see."

He went out to his car, limping over the pavement in unlaced patent leathers and drove away without thinking of her. But Francine was happy and did not cry in bed that night.

The end of Chez Blomme off Bond Street and the appearance of Ricci Blomme's Temple of Beauty in Oxford Street provoked a fashionable stir.

Old clients tried everything from bribery to blackmail to prevent the cheapening of the Process and, such is the spite of women, even the police had many anonymous complaints.

Once again it was the simple excellence of the Process itself which saved the situation. A single treatment lasted for six months and no woman who had tasted the fruits of loveliness for so long could face a return to natural insignificance for the sake of a trip to Ricci's Temple.

Ricci rejoiced. He had plenty of money and saw himself a mighty public benefactor. He went ahead with enthusiasm.

Francine was happy, her position as Ricci's personal assistant gave her a new importance and she saw him every day.

The organisation of the business was itself a miracle. Ricci set about it with that fearless common sense which is so often a by-product of genius. He conducted classes of picked assistants, instructing and inspiring them even while they laughed at his enthusiasm.

His private eyebrow treatment, alone worth a small fortune, he divulged happily, alternately coaxing and bullying his small army into his own methods. He expanded, overworked and was sublimely content.

Francine watched and adored him.

George Briesemann appeared during the first month of the new venture when the beauty trade of London and Paris was seething with indignation and alarm, since Ricci tore up all offers for the Process indiscriminately and took a childish delight in throwing out importunate business visitors personally.

Briesemann was a sleek, soft-voiced young man with a keen clever face and large, shining, light brown eyes. There was an efficiency about his work which should have warned his employer, but Ricci was too happy to be suspicious of anybody and he liked George.

The only secret which Ricci kept religiously was the Lotion Blomme which was the main basis of the Process. His method of preserving it was simple in the extreme. Since its secret lay in the blending and not in the actual ingredients, he did not fear analysis but merely took the precaution of manufacturing it himself in the kitchenette of his flat, bringing it by car to the shop in the mornings in gallon-size stone beer jars.

Sometimes when he was very rushed, he took Francine home with him to help. This signal honour gratified Francine, but only because it gave her more time with him and it did not occur to her to be surprised the Ricci should trust her.

George Briesemann, on the other hand, was tremendously impressed and Francine found him more attentive than any man she had ever known. She was a little flattered and when he looked at her with soft, pathetic eyes she felt a twinge of dangerous pity for him.

Probably the whole thing would never have happened if it had not been for the window. The Temple of Beauty had been built as a café and, although the inside had been converted when Ricci took the place over, he had been far too occupied with the immediate necessities of his business to worry about the façade.

Curiously, it did not matter. The Process Blomme was its own advertisement.

However, unfortunately, once the internal arrangements of the Temple were in good working order, Ricci became aware of the large plate-glass window and it was his undoing.

He stood out in the street early one Friday morning and

regarded it thoughtfully. At that moment it was simply hung with purple velvet and contained only the small silver sign from the other shop. Ricci sighed. It was inadequate. It was mean. It was a snub to his genius.

He stood out on the pavement for some little time, sublimely unconscious of the passers-by. His short legs were straddled, his great head was thrown back and his eyes were screwed up in an ecstasy of creation.

Suddenly, the idea came to him as he had known it would; a notion of genius, beautiful in its simplicity. He went slowly up to his office and sent for Francine.

She came at once, unaware of the approaching crisis. She was a little breathless on entering, having had to hurry up the staircase, and there was a suggestion of colour in her cheeks.

Ricci walked slowly across the room, took her by the hand and led her to the window. Then he looked at her.

The great moments of life, if long awaited, are apt to be disappointing and marred by unexpected reactions in oneself. Francine found herself alarmed lest her knees should give way and she suffered a childish impulse to cover her face with her hands now that those bright eyes were fixed searchingly upon her, taking in every curve and feature with professional interest.

It was happening. The dream was materialising. She was terrified.

"Uh!" said Ricci after what had promised to be an unending silence. He ran a short finger over her eyebrows and tested the texture of her hair at the roots. "Good," he continued and strode down the room laughing. He appeared to be delighted.

Francine leaned against the windowsill and wished her heart would stop beating so clumsily.

Ricci sat down at his desk, swinging his short legs and crowing with suppressed amusement.

"I'll show that Graustadt," he said. "Publicity — he don' know anything. I'll show 'im."

Francine did not seek to hurry him, although her heart was bursting. She stood looking at him dumbly, waiting for him to speak.

"Tell you what, Francine," he went on at last. "I won't tell anyone 'bout this till I got it done. Ricci's going to surprise 'em. You come round to the flat on Sunday and I'll fix you, see?"

"Fix me?" She stood very still, her dark eyes burning in her small pale face.

Ricci beamed. "That's right. I fix you up. Your face is all right, Francine. It's good. You'll look all right. Run 'long now. Don' tell anyone. You'll be my masterpiece. You'll see."

Francine stumbled from the room. Briesemann found her crumpled in a corner of the enormous linen cupboard half an hour later. He picked her up and sat her on a chair, watching her with sharp intelligence behind the gentleness in his eyes.

When she had stopped trembling, he put his question.

"Had a row with Blomme?"

The inquiry was so unexpected that she did not wonder at his eagerness.

"Oh, no," she said. "Not at all."

Briesemann's eyes grew moist.

"You're such a sweet kid," he said, dropping his voice a tone or so. "It's mean of him not to let you have the treatment. I'd do it for you myself if I could get the stuff. You could also make some, couldn't you?"

She began to laugh, and he paused aghast, terrified that his approach had been too crude. When she said nothing, however, he went on cautiously.

"He'll wear himself out, superintending each skinning himself, twenty to thirty a day. It's more than a man can stand."

"He always worked very hard," said Francine and stood up.

Briesemann laid a hand on her shoulder.

"He's not the only man in the world," he said. "I'd like to take you for a ride in the country on Sunday."

The words were not eloquent but his round liquid eyes were soft and contained an unspoken longing, while Francine was both feminine and inexperienced. She touched his hand lightly.

"I'm very sorry, George, really very sorry," she said earnestly and hurried away.

Briesemann, who flattered himself that he understood women, was completely fogged. That evening, when he dropped in to see his brother-in-law Louis Bernstein, president of the Bernstein and Fleischmann Beauty Range Ltd, he said so.

Ricci sent the car for Francine two hours before the appointed time on Sunday morning and Petersen, the chauffeur, had almost unbearably gratifying news for her.

"Beside himself," he said swinging the car into Shaftesbury Avenue. "Like a kid with a game on. If he's told me to fetch you at twelve once he's told me a dozen times."

Francine did not speak. She was sitting very still, savouring the precious minutes like a connoisseur breathing over a rare brandy. It was happening. It was coming true. Miser-like, she guarded each sweet second of her joy.

Ricci received her like an excited dog. He was so delighted with his glorious idea that he could hardly contain himself. Before she had taken her coat off, he had dragged her into his spare room, where the whole paraphernalia had been installed.

"Sit down, Francine, sit down," he commanded. "I've been waiting for you. Now I don' want no mirrors, see? It's going to be a surprise to you, same as everyone. You're going to congratulate me, Francine."

Francine moved slowly. She was still conscious of a need to conserve her happiness, storing it away scrap by scrap so that its full avalanche should not overwhelm her.

The mood made her a trifle stupid, but Ricci did not notice it. He forgot her and concentrated upon her face. The time passed slowly and gloriously for the girl. She dared hardly breathe while his quick plump fingers played over her face and neck.

It was a long-drawn-out ecstasy, like the moment before the play begins, stretched into hours of swooning expectation.

While the plasters were on and he was dressing her hair, drawing it all to one side, Ricci began to sing. Francine's heart leapt painfully. When Ricci sang things were going well. He had a curious repertoire — "On with the Motley," "Red Sails in the Sunset" and a portion of the "Song of the Flea," all sung execrably and with enormous power.

It was nearly four and Francine had eaten nothing since a seven o'clock breakfast, when at last he paused and stepped back from her. The cosmetic stage had come and gone, and he had just applied the finishing touches with a pad of virgin cotton wool. Francine dared not look at him. Now that the crucial moment had arrived, the instant when the reward of beauty actually became due, she felt sick and faint and terrified.

Ricci threw down the wool and clasped his hands.

"Ha!" he exclaimed explosively.

Glancing at him she saw that his eyes were dancing.

"I'll show that Graustadt," he said. "Wait. Stay where you are. I'll get you a mirror and you'll laugh at him, too. Publicity...I'll show that fellow!"

He went out, to return with a slender pier-glass from the bedroom.

"Don' look, Francine. Don' look till I say."

There was a childish thrill in his voice and her arms ached to hold him. She closed her eyes obediently.

"Now!"

Francine looked up.

One of the peculiarities of the Process Blomme was its star-tling effect upon the colour of the skin. It genuinely gave a soft, pearly, radiant complexion to any woman, sallow or red, and was both unmistakable and lovely.

"Well?" demanded Ricci in ecstasy. "Well?"

Francine did not take her eyes from the mirror. She presented a remarkable spectacle. One half of her face, divided by a perpendicular line from the peak of her forehead to the tip of her thymus bone, was as beautiful as Ricci's art could make it. Her dark eyebrow was plucked into a perfect arch. Half her nose, half her mouth were miracles of gentle elegance and her skin was virgin cream.

The other side of her face was as it had ever been, sallow, blurred and indeterminate.

Ricci had done his work with his customary attention to detail. One side of her hair was dressed as only he could dress it; the other was drab and untidy.

The effect was startlingly bizarre, the very contrast lending an added strength to each aspect. In life Francine had never looked so unprepossessing, in dreams she had never looked so deliriously beautiful.

"Now we will have a dress made, one side fashionable, svelte and alluring, the other — not so good. You shall wear it and sit in the window and what will that Graustadt say then, eh?"

Ricci's voice was jubilant.

"He will revile himself, Francine. 'That Ricci knows something,' he will say that."

Francine rose slowly to her feet. There was a thunder in her ears and her limbs were heavy.

Ricci went on prattling excitedly.

"You will have a gold chair, gold one side, deal the other and you shall wear odd shoes — that's good, eh? Where are you going, Francine?"

From the doorway she paused and looked at him. The light fell on the beautiful half of her face and he saw a strange new Francine who was so different from the old that a chill assailed him. It was the first symptom of the doubt that was to undermine his faith in the Process.

Still she did not speak, and he frowned with momentary misgiving.

"Come 'ere," he said. "Listen to me, I got to tell you what to do in the window tomorrow. What's the matter with you? Come 'ere."

Francine went out of the room and out of the flat, down into the street. She held a handkerchief over one half of her face as do women who have been scarred. Because the world had ended, and the floods had engulfed her, she clutched at the first straw to present itself. She telephoned George Briesemann.

That evening Ricci had the shock of his lifetime. He paced up and down the living room of the flat in his stockinged feet while the air still tingled with the force of his visitor's opening peroration.

Briesemann, who in his own opinion had acquitted himself rather well, lounged against the armchair by the fire, his face alive and interested and his long thin fingers drumming on the upholstered back.

Ricci thrust his hand through his coarse hair.

"I'm sorry, George, you know. I'm sorry," he said helplessly. "I didn't know about you and Francine. I didn't know about her being your girl. I never thought she'd mind. I thought she'd be pleased. Francine's worked for me a long time now, you know that."

Briesemann allowed his tongue to pass over his full lips. He was not aiming at reconciliation and Ricci's reception of his outburst had been unexpected.

"You won't get out of it that way, Blomme," he said passionately. "Francine is my girl and I was going to pay you to give her that treatment when we could afford it. I don't want any woman made into an advertising guy."

Ricci sat down with a jolt on the hard chair by the table. He was aware of the arrival of several new ideas that needed assimilating.

Briesemann began to shout. "You'll put that girl's face right this evening and that's the last you'll ever see of her or me — get that into your head. I could get damages off you, d'you know that? Any monkey stuff with me and I tell you I don't care who you are, I'll..."

"George!"

Ricci put up a hand as though to deflect a blow.

"George, I'm sorry. I feel kind of sick," he continued with genuine mystification. He placed a finger on his solar plexus. "I feel sort of sick 'ere. Maybe I'm going to be ill."

"You'll do Francine's face tonight if you're dying," said Briesemann. "I've got her in a taxi outside."

Ricci threw out his hands. "I'll do it, George. I'd have done it any time if she'd mentioned it. I didn't think of it."

"You never think of anything but your damned Process."

"No," said Ricci simply. "No, George, I don't. Go and fetch Francine. I'll fix her up all right."

When the other man reached the threshold he added blankly: "I didn't know you and Francine were...that way, George?"

"I told you, you don't notice anything," said Briesemann over his shoulder.

The second half of Francine's transformation took place in grim silence with George Briesemann watching every stage with alert, intelligent eyes. Francine was so quiet that she seemed scarcely to breathe and Ricci, who had begun with clumsy apologies, sank into moroseness very early in the proceedings.

It was only when it was all done, and the miracle was complete that Francine trusted herself to speak. She looked up from the only half-familiar face in the mirror and met Ricci's eyes.

"Thank you," she said.

The great hour had come and passed. The dream had turned out to be but a dream. It was cold and quiet in the room. Briesemann scented danger.

"Good enough," he said briskly. "Come along, Francine, we've finished here. You've seen the last of us, Blomme. Come on, we won't waste the great inventor's time."

Francine gazed at Ricci. Her eyes were tragic and imploring, her face rigid and without expression.

Ricci passed his hand over his forehead and regarded his handiwork with growing dubiety.

"It don't look so good to me," he said. "I don' see what's wrong but it don' look so good."

Francine's newly brightened eyes were tearful and Briesemann took her arm.

"It's okay by me," he said. "And that's what counts, Mr Blomme. Come along, Francine."

After they had gone, Ricci wandered up and down the flat, his hair tufty and on end. The doubt in his mind was increasing, and from time to time he went back to the spare room and examined the lotions he had used.

At three in the morning, Petersen found him in the kitchenette at work on a new brew.

"It's not so good," he said in reply to startled questioning. "I don' know what it is. Something is wrong. It's not so good. I got to see about it."

"Your perishing Process!" said Petersen and went back to bed.

With the departure of Francine for Bernstein and Fleischmann's Beauty Range Ltd, a new phase of the beauty war began. Francine was now lovely. Her natural daintiness was accentuated by the new beauty of her face. Bernstein's brought out a new line with her photograph in colours on the wrappers and the story went around that the Process Blomme had been repeated at last.

Later it was rumoured that Bernstein's were not satisfied with the blending of the new lotion. Either the girl was a fool, or she had double-crossed them, they said; no one could determine which.

Francine knew the truth and told it to George Briesemann.

"Ricci is the secret," she said. "It is like an omelette."

And, although he alternatively bullied and coaxed her, she seemed incapable of being more explicit. However, Bernstein's had Francine's face and they had a lotion complete with careful directions which were too complicated for either the general public or the small beauty specialists to follow.

Some experts introduced a process based on the Bernstein lotion with considerable success, but the general feeling was that something had gone wrong with the new-faces-for-old campaign.

Chief among the scaremongers was Ricci himself. It seemed to him that with Francine's transformation some of the virtue of the Process had departed. He could not understand it. He noticed it in every new case he handled.

"It don' look so good to me," became a catchphrase in the Temple.

No one else noticed the difference at first but Ricci's dissidence was infectious. Moreover, his enthusiasm had been the mainspring of his business and now its resilience was gone.

Some of the assistants began to think that they too saw a change.

The appointments did not begin to fall off immediately and when they did it was largely because of flaws in the organisation. There were carelessnesses and quarrels among the assistants.

Ricci was despairing. After some months of growing dismay he appointed a manager and went to see a doctor. The professional man prescribed immediate rest. Ricci heaved a sigh, deserted the Temple and, locking himself in his flat, began to experiment all over again.

It was rumoured in the beauty world that he had gone mad.

Francine bore it for a long time.

It was not until the rumours concerning the decline of the Temple of Beauty were terrifying and Petersen reported that Ricci had not eaten for three days or spoken for ten that she decided to act.

In four months she had made the fundamental discovery that if beauty be not a key to love it is at least the passport to many audacities.

She left the hotel where Bernstein's had decreed she should live, as a walking advertisement for their product, and presented herself at the flat.

Petersen admitted her, and she went into the spare-room laboratory which was in much the same condition that Ricci's bedroom at Madame Sousa's had been in, so long ago that she had almost forgotten it. Ricci was sitting at the work bench in trousers and singlet, his hands in his pockets. He looked crumpled and there were grey streaks in his hair.

Francine went in quietly and sat down. She did not speak but when he turned, she looked at him anxiously.

"Eh?" he said. "Hello, Francine. There's something wrong with the Process. I can't find what it is. The women don' look so good to me. They're not beautiful any more, Francine."

He spoke jerkily and there was a glaze of weariness over his eyes. He did not appear to realise that it was their first meeting for months.

Still she did not speak, and he shook his shaggy head mournfully.

"They were all right. They used to look good. You remember, Francine, they used to be okay. Now — I don' know — they're not right. They don' look so well. I can't do anything. I'm in the dark. I don' know what's wrong."

She made her request and he shrugged his shoulders.

"Oh, I'll do it for you if you like but it won't be so good. Something's gone wrong with the Process, I tell you. I'm done, Francine. I'm finished."

As he set about the work wearily with tired fingers which yet had not lost their deftness, he went on talking.

"You were my first failure. Your face is not so good. I didn't hardly recognise you when you came in. There's something wrong with the Process. I looked at you that night and you weren't beautiful, Francine. That fellow George, he didn't see it. But I did. I saw it at once, and it was wrong. How is George?"

"I haven't seen him for three months. He's gone to the Manchester branch." Francine's voice came faintly through the linen mask.

"Huh? I thought you was..." He paused and added politely, "married to him?"

"No."

"He treat you badly, Francine?" Ricci was diffident.

"No, there was never... He just got me a different job, that's all."

"Is that so? You mean you was never his girl?" Ricci's interest sounded impersonal but keen.

"No, never. Of course not."

"Huh." This time the sound expressed satisfaction. "That's good, eh? Now I do your hair, I think, while the mask does the work."

He busied himself for some time and seemed engrossed, but it became evident at last that he had not entirely dismissed Briesemann from his mind.

"Eh, that George," he remarked at last. "I don' like that fellow."

There was another long pause as he sighed and blew above her head with gusty dissatisfaction.

"I'm tired, Francine. There's something wrong with the Process. You'll see it for yourself when I take this off. I'll get it right, you know, but it takes time. I've been here months now. I can't find out what's wrong."

She made a stifled conciliatory sound and he hesitated, running her fine black hair through his fingers before he spoke.

"You don' want to work for Bernstein," he said at last. "You want to work for Ricci Blomme. I'm not finished, Francine. I'm all right. You want to work for me. Work for me up here."

"Here?"

"Yes." Ricci blurred his words. "I need a girl. I need a girl like you, Francine. Look here, you live here and work for me. You'll like it, Francine. I want you here with me, see? I'm sorry about the window. The idea wasn't so good. I'm not so clever at publicity, maybe. Come back and work for me."

The speech bubbled out of his mouth and he came round to stand before her, a wildly dishevelled figure with a four-days' growth of beard and round childlike eyes.

Behind the mask Francine was still.

"Come on, Francine. You stay here, eh?"

He was frankly wheedling now, and he took off the mask and threw on the soothing fomentation of cream as he talked, massaging the cool mass into her tingling skin.

"I've missed you, Francine. I send for you and you weren't there. Then I remember you'd had the Process and it wasn't so good. Come back 'ere till I get it right again. Just till I get it right. What do you say? Marry me and live 'ere if you like."

Francine took the towel from his arm and wiped her face. There were highlights on her cheekbones and on the tip of her small nose. Her eyes were clear of cosmetics and her hair was disarranged.

"I love you Ricci," she said.

"Love?" echoed Ricci as though he had never heard the word before. "Love, eh?"

Gradually, however, its significance began to dawn upon him.

"Love, eh?" he repeated with growing delight. "Eh, eh, Francine, come 'ere to me."

When he released her, she was breathless, and he stepped back to look at her.

She was radiant. Shining skin and disordered hair could not disguise it. Her face was alive. She was transfigured, glorious.

Ricci gaped.

"The Process!" he said huskily, his eyes bulging. "The Process, it has returned! By God, look Francine, it has returned! I, Ricci Blomme, I have discovered it! I — eh, Francine, come over 'ere."

He took her to a mirror.

"Look," he commanded, incoherent with excitement. "See what

I do for you, eh, Francine? My darling, my little thin one, I make you beautiful. I did it! I, Ricci Blomme."

Francine put her arms round his neck.

"Yes, you did it," she said. "You did it — my dear."

Ricci sang.

THE BLACK TENT

L ord Currier's maternal Uncle John was in the Cabinet and, as he was not slow to tell anyone who could be persuaded to listen, his finger was on the pulse of the world. This remarkable facility clearly did not absorb all his time or energy for, whenever he had the chance, the distinguished old gentleman was eager to quit the Olympian heights to interfere in the affairs of his more important relatives.

At eleven o'clock one evening in the library of his future mother-in-law's house in Clarges Street, Lord Currier, Tommy to his closer acquaintances, was confiding his relief to his friend Albert Campion. The two were snatching a few moments' respite and whiskey-and-sodas whilst on the floor below them, in the rose-decorated ballroom, a ball was in progress in honour of his fiancée, the incomparable Roberta. The music of the Red Hot Cobblers came up to them. Lord Currier set down his glass and blinked at Campion.

"It was a damned near go," he said solemnly. "The old man's a bachelor of the worst type. I had to tell him I was in love, not buying a horse. You see, it wasn't only her grandfather who got under his skin; he's been reading the Sunday papers and got all

sorts of wild ideas about women into his head — flighty, dangerous, serpents in disguise, you know the sort of thing. Of course,
when I persuaded him to meet Roberta he came to his senses, but
it was a near thing."

Mr Campion settled his lean form on the arm of a gigantic
leather chair and adjusted his horn-rimmed spectacles.

"Uncle John is something of a power, I take it?" he murmured.

Tommy Currier's mild brown eyes opened to their widest.

"Good lord, yes," he said, in some surprise that the matter
should have been questioned. "Uncle John is the final and ultimate
word. Uncle John pulls the strings. If I'm to have the career in the
Diplomatic which my old man has set his heart on, what Uncle
John says goes every time."

"I see. And now, fortunately, Roberta goes?"

The younger man sighed ecstatically.

"She does, bless her," he said. "I must cut along back to the
dance or she'll be looking for me. They've got a fortune teller chap
down there. She wants me to consult him and I'm in that state
when I'll do anything, anything she asks. Don't hurry. Finish your
drink and come down when you feel like it."

He trotted out of the room, his wide sleek shoulders betraying
all the excitement which he kept so successfully out of his round
affable face. He was so completely, not to say dementedly, happy
that he made his companion feel a trifle elderly.

Left to himself, Mr Campion set down his glass and reflected
that Uncle John was an anachronism in an age when a grandfather who had made a fortune out of frozen meat should rightly
be nothing but a valuable asset to any pretty young woman.

The music from the ballroom was not inviting and the library
was cool and pleasant. True, the books in the glass-fronted cabi-
nets did not look as though they had ever been read, and the great
desk in the centre of the carpet was obviously never used, but the
light was gently diffused and the atmosphere peaceful. Campion
was weary. In the company of his friend, Superintendent Stanis-

laus Oates of the Central Criminal Branch, he had spent the best part of three nights that week in a grey office in Scotland Yard going over the documents in a particularly exasperating insurance fraud. For three days he had been out of his bed for twenty hours in every twenty-four so that now the quiet depths of the green armchair were irresistibly inviting. He slid into it gratefully. The chair enveloped and concealed him, and he lay still.

A little over half an hour later he awoke quietly with every sense alert. He opened his eyes cautiously and, in the angle of the chair-arm, he glimpsed the heel of a green satin slipper on the carpet. Its owner was fighting with the bottom drawer of the bureau in the corner behind him and was doing her unsuccessful best to be as quiet about the business as was possible.

Long practice had taught Mr Campion to move soundlessly. Now he pulled himself up slowly and peered over the arm of the chair.

The girl kneeling before the bureau was forcing the catch of the bottom drawer back with a long brass paper-knife. She was young, that was the first thing he noticed about her, but then he saw that her red hair hung loosely round a small and shapely head, and immediately he noticed that her green dress floated gracefully about a slender, childish figure. He watched her with polite interest and then he saw her slide the drawer open an inch or so, slip in a small hand and draw out what appeared to be a flat package. This she wrapped guiltily in a big georgette handkerchief.

Deeming that the moment had come, Mr Campion coughed apologetically.

The girl in the green dress stiffened and there was a moment of painful silence, then she turned and rose quietly to her feet. Campion found himself looking into a small, intelligent face which in a year or so would blossom inevitably into beauty. He judged her to be at the most fifteen years old. Her face was now very red, and her grey-green eyes were angry and alarmed, but she was not without courage and her first remark was as bald as it was unexpected, and it had in it a strong element of truth which silenced Campion.

"It's nothing to do with you," she said, then banging the drawer shut she fled the room before Campion could stop her, leaving the paper-knife on the carpet.

Mr Campion pulled himself together and went quietly down to the ballroom.

He was mildly startled and just a little conscious of his own invidious position. He was a guest of the prospective son-in-law of the house and as such should have been doing his duty on the dance floor and not sleeping peacefully beside a tantalus in the library. Yet he was aware that young women who open bureau drawers with paper-knives and run off with mysterious packages wrapped in georgette handkerchiefs constitute a responsibility which cannot be altogether ignored. He went to look for the girl.

The white and gilt ballroom was hot and smelt like a florist's shop. Everyone Mr Campion had ever met round a dinner table seemed to be present with her daughter, but of the little girl in the green dress there was no trace at all. Once he thought he caught a glimpse of her small, heart-shaped face across the room, but on struggling through the throng toward this young woman he discovered that he was mistaken and that it was not she but Roberta Pelham herself, radiant and excited, her arm through the arm of her fiancé.

Mr Campion turned into an anteroom to find air and was thereupon astonished to be confronted by nothing less than a black velvet tent, hung with gilt fringe and topped impressively by a brass Directoire eagle. The tent was an incongruous contraption in this high-ceilinged Georgian room, and he stood blinking at it for some seconds before it dawned on him that this must be booth of the fortune teller Thomas had been talking about.

Mr Campion was turning away when the tent curtain parted

and old Lady Frinton, who by his reckoning should have known a great deal better at her age, came out in a flutter.

"Oh, my dear!" she exclaimed, pouncing on him happily. "My *dear!* The creature's too astonishing! Phillida was inspired to engage him. She took my advice, of course. I told her it needs something original to make these young people affairs faintly tolerable for adults. Come and sit down and I'll tell you every-thing he told me — or nearly everything — the stupid man. So amusing!"

She chuckled reminiscently, seized his arm and was leading him away when her old eyes, which were sharp and shrewd enough in all conscience, caught his interested expression and she swung round to see what had attracted him.

The floating skirt of a green dress flickered for a moment at the further end of the room and a heart-shaped face surmounted by auburn hair appeared for an instant, only to catch sight of Mr Campion and disappear again. The Dowager Lady Frinton raised her eyebrows.

"Albert!" she said. "My dear boy! A child? Well, it's an extraordinary thing to me but I've noticed it over and over again. You clever men are absolutely devastated by immaturity, aren't you? Still, fifteen...dear boy, is it wise?"

"Do you know who she is?" Campion forced the inquiry in edgeways but did not for an instant dam the flow of chatter for which the old lady was justly famous.

"Who she is?" she exclaimed, her eyes crinkling. "My dear man, you don't mean to say you haven't even met! But how touchingly romantic! I thought you young people managed these things very differently nowadays. Still, this is charming, tell me more. You just looked at each other, I suppose? Dear me, it takes me back years."

Campion regarded her helplessly. She was like some elderly, fat, white kitten, he thought suddenly, all fluff and wide smile.

"Who is she?" he repeated doggedly.

"Why, the child, of course of..." Lady Frinton was infuriating.

"Little what's-her-name — Jennifer, isn't it? My dear man, don't stand looking at me like a fish. You know perfectly well who I mean. Roberta's sister, Phillida's youngest daughter. Yes, Jennifer, that's the name. So pretty. Devonshire, isn't it?"

"A daughter?" Campion groped through this spate of scattered information. "She lives here, then?"

"Of course she lives here. Where else should she live but with her mother? A child of fifteen living alone? Good heavens, whatever next?"

Her ladyship's eyebrows seemed in danger of disappearing altogether, but she rattled on.

"She's a charming little thing, I believe, although I've never had any patience with school-children myself. Still, far too young for you. Put it out of your mind, dear boy. Let me see, what was I going to tell you? Oh, about the fortune teller, of course. Quite a remarkable man. A psychometrist. Fortunately I'm never indiscreet, but really, some of the things he told me about people I knew..."

Her squeaky voice rose and fell, and it occurred to Mr Campion that she must have told the seer quite as much as ever he told her. While she was talking, he had leisure to wonder why Miss Jennifer Pelham had chosen the middle of a party to force open a locked drawer in the library of her own home, and why above all she should have been so infernally guilty about it.

The matter did not seem of great importance, however, and he was considering how long it would be before he could decently take his leave and go home to bed when a more or less lucid paragraph in Lady Frinton's endless recitation caught his attention.

"He took my ring and put it into an envelope. I put the envelope under the crystal and then he looked in and told me the most astonishing things about my mother. Wasn't that amazing?"

"Your ring?" inquired Mr Campion.

The old lady looked at him as though she thought he was deficient.

"I believe you're still thinking about that child," she declared, adding spitefully, "And at your age! I've been explaining. Cagliostro is a psychometrist. You give him something that belonged to someone dead, dead or elsewhere anyway, and he tells you all about them. It's remarkable, truly remarkable."

"Cagliostro?" inquired Campion, temporarily out of his depth.

Lady Frinton threw up her tiny hands in exasperation.

"Bless the man, he's delirious," she said. "Cagliostro the Second is the fortune teller. Cagliostro is the man in the tent over there. Go and see him for yourself. I can't be bothered with you if you don't use your mind at all. You young people ought to take up yoga. Come and see me and I'll put you on to a very good man."

She trotted off happily and Campion heaved a sigh of relief, yet, having a naturally inquisitive disposition, he did not go home immediately but wandered across the room to peer into the black tent before making his way back to the ballroom.

The scene within the tent was much as he had expected. A strong overhead light shone down upon a small, black, velvet-covered table which supported among other things a red satin cushion and a large crystal ball; but he was not prepared for the man who smiled at him over an unimpeachable shirt front. This Cagliostro was not the usual sleek huckster with the bright eyes and swagger which the credulous public has come to expect in its seers, but a surprisingly large man with thin fluffy hair and prominent, cold, light eyes. He did not speak but indicated the consultant's chair very slowly with a large, fin-like hand.

Campion shook his head hastily and hurried away. It was a trivial incident, but it left him oddly uncomfortable. He was even glad to get back to the ballroom.

He stayed for another three-quarters of an hour and kept a weather eye open for the younger daughter of the house, who still interested him, but she was not in the room and he did not see her again until he was actually in the street on his way home.

It was a fine night and as he came out into the warm darkness, he decided to walk the few steps from Clarges Street to his Piccadilly home. His way took him down the side of the house, which was on a corner, and as he passed a ground floor window sprang into light and he saw Jennifer standing by the door. She remained very still for a moment, her back against the door. There was conscious drama in her pose and Campion paused on the pavement in some astonishment. As he watched she tore open a white envelope and drew out a small flat package. Immediately all trace of theatre disappeared, and she became a very real girl in very real alarm.

Jennifer shook out the package and Campion saw that it was a single sheet of newspaper. For some reason the sight of it appalled the younger Miss Pelham. She held it at arm's length and raised a white, startled face to the blank window. And that was all.

The next moment something, presumably a sound from behind the door, caused her to start guiltily. She crumpled both newspaper and envelope into a ball and dropped it into a waste-paper basket. A second later the room was dark again.

As Mr Campion walked on down the street he blinked behind his spectacles. The unworthy notion that the younger sister of Lord Currier's prospective bride was off her little red head occurred to him, but he rejected it and for some time as he moved on, he was engrossed in idle speculation.

However, by the time he reached Bottle Street he had decided that whatever the mystery might be it was mercifully no affair of his, and he went to bed soothed by that curiously mistaken notion.

He heard no more of the Pelhams for nearly three weeks and had all but forgotten the tempestuous figure in the green dress when, one morning as he sat at his desk, a note was brought to him with a visiting card on which was engraved simply "Mr Waldo Allen, New York." The note was more instructive.

Dear Campion [wrote the Superintendent],

Mr Allen has a difficult problem. While we are anxious to give him every assistance, we have no information of the kind he needs. It came into my head that there is a faint chance that you may know something, so I am taking the liberty of sending him along.

Yours ever,

SO

Campion grinned. The good policeman's difficulty could not have been more lucidly expressed had he added a postscript: "I cannot get rid of this chap politely, old boy. See what you can do."

Yet when Waldo Allen, the Wall Street financier, came into the room his personality immediately captivated his host.

Allen was a large, thoughtful man with a natural dignity and an air of authority which was both unconscious and impressive. He stood, stooping a little in the doorway, peering at Campion with bright, worried eyes which were faintly shy.

"This is very kind of you," he said at last in a slow, quiet voice, and he seated himself in the armchair before the desk. He cleared his throat, hesitated, and suddenly smiled.

"I am aware that I may sound to you as though I'm crazy," he murmured, "but this is my problem. I'm looking for a skunk, Mr Campion, and eventually I'm going to get him. I have some influence with the authorities on the other side, and your people have been kindly and considerate. With their help I think I may be able to deal with the man I want, once I can locate him, but I've got to find him first. That's my problem. Can you help me?"

Campion sat with his head a little on one side and his pale eyes quizzical.

"A skunk?" he inquired dubiously.

The American nodded and the expression in his bright eyes was by no means amused.

"A skunk," he said soberly. "The lowest animal I ever hope to come across. I've never seen him, but I know he exists, and I have reason to believe he's in England. Have you ever been married, Mr Campion?"

The abruptness of the question was disconcerting, and the visitor seemed disappointed when Mr Campion shook his head. Waldo Allen leant forward in his chair.

"I have," he said. "Two years ago I married one of the most charming girls in the world. She was young and very ignorant, and like a fool I took her straight away from her parents' home in South Carolina to a penthouse in New York. I gave her everything that she wanted and introduced her to my friends. Then I got on with my work and left her to settle into life in the smart city set. I can't tell you how bitterly I've reproached myself for doing just that. If I'd had any sense, I'd have realised that she needed more protection than my money, and just my money, could give her. She should have had my entire attention. I should have realised that the extraordinary simplicity and childishness which I loved in her was a danger as much as it was a charm."

He paused, and the sophisticated Mr Campion found himself unexpectedly moved by the genuine pain in the quiet, unemotional voice. Waldo Allen looked up.

"Six months ago she threw herself from the roof garden surrounding our penthouse," he said slowly. "There was a lot of hush-hush business and I believe the DA satisfied himself that it was an accident. It was not. I wish to God it had been. That skunk had blackmailed her until she hadn't a cent or a jewel to her name and she was afraid to come to me for more."

He rose abruptly and turned down the room.

"I won't bother you with that angle," he said at last. "You must take it that it was my fault. If I'd realised what a child she was, then the whole tragedy would never have happened. But I didn't. I gave her money instead of understanding. What I have to tell you is what we discovered after her death. She had sold everything that was her own, Mr Campion, her bank balance was nil. Large irregular withdrawals in cash told the story pretty clearly. I was nearly off my head. I couldn't understand it. I couldn't imagine what the child could have had to hide. But I didn't know her, you see. I didn't realise her youth or her inexperience."

Campion nodded. It was impossible not to be sorry for this big, quiet man who kept such a tight rein on his well-nigh intolerable grief.

"Did you ever discover what it was?" he inquired.

The American smiled bitterly. "I've got a pretty shrewd idea," he said. "Sylvia had a personal maid, Dorothy, a coloured girl her own age. The girl had come up with her from South Carolina. After the tragedy she broke down and told all she knew. Apparently, Sylvia had kept some letters. The sentimental mementos of a boy-and-girl love affair which had fizzled out before I put in an appearance. Dorothy was not at all sure what had happened, but she thought that someone had got hold of those letters and had convinced Sylvia that I would read a great deal more into them than ever they had contained. To prevent me seeing them my wife ruined herself, worked herself into a state of nervous collapse and finally killed herself. I must get my hands on that man, Mr Campion. He doesn't deserve to live."

The younger man was silent. So often in his career he had heard similar tales that he could not now doubt this grim little story. The clever blackmailer who picks the right victim need discover very little which is truly reprehensible on which to base his threats.

Campion stirred.

"You never traced the man?"

"Never. I've spent six months on it and I've barely a clue. Sylvia went everywhere and met all the usual people, yet she was often alone. Dorothy cannot help; the girl knows no more than I do now. I've just two things to go on and they're slender enough, God knows."

He came up to the desk as he spoke and stood looking down gravely, his big hands resting on the polished wood.

"The first clue brought me to England. Her maid says that once Sylvia burst into tears when they were alone together and said then that she wished it were July. Dorothy asked her why, and Sylvia sat staring in front of her, a terrified expression in her eyes. 'He always goes to England in July,' she said, but she wouldn't explain herself and, of course, the maid didn't like to press her. That's one of my clues. I know it's slender but I'm clutching at straws."

Campion's quick smile was reassuring.

"And the other clue?" he inquired gently.

Waldo Allen straightened his back.

"Just before my wife died," he began softly, "she came into my study where I sat writing. I was very busy and, God forgive me, I didn't look at her. She put her arms round my neck, kissed me and whispered something. The next moment she had gone through the French windows, across the roof garden to her death."

His voice quivered dangerously, but he controlled himself and went on steadily enough.

"Again and again I've gone over those whispered words in my mind, but I can't get any sense out of them. I heard them distinctly. Sylvia said: 'Forgive me. It's written in the ink. He must have seen it all the time.' That was all. Before I could take my mind off my work and ask her what she was talking about she'd gone."

Campion drew a desk-pad toward him and on it wrote the strange disjointed sentences in his neat, academic hand.

"'It is written in ink,'" he read it aloud slowly. "Are you sure of that?"

The man with the bright, worried eyes nodded gravely.

"I'm certain," he said heavily. "Those three phrases will remain in my mind until I die. At one time I came close to persuading myself that they were evidence to the unhinged state of her brain, but now that I've seen her pitiful bank account and her empty jewel case I can't reconcile myself to any theory of that sort. My wife was not mad, Mr Campion. To all intents and purposes she was murdered. Now you understand why I've got to get my hands on that brute. Can you help me?"

Campion hesitated. From the moment when this strange, likeable personality had invaded his study to pour out a story no less tragic because it was deliberately understated, an idea had been knocking at the door of his mind. On the face of it, Mr Allen's request was absurd. Even in his most self-satisfied moments Mr Campion did not presume to consider himself a magician and to undertake to look for a blackmailer who might or might not be in England and toward whose identification there was not a shred of evidence, was not the sort of quest to appeal to anyone with a reasonable opinion of his own powers.

Yet there was something very curious about the story he had just heard, and as he sat at his desk, his eyes thoughtful behind his spectacles, suddenly he realised that there was about it a startling and uncomfortable note of familiarity. The discovery rattled him. It was like hearing a tune for the second time and not being able to place its title.

The American rose.

"I fear it's too much of a tall order," he said wearily, "Your police were very polite, but I could see they thought it was asking for the moon. For all I know, the blackguard I'm searching for may be the man who waits on me in a restaurant, the stranger who sits next to me in the theatre, or the fellow who walks past me in the street. I can't blame you if you laugh at me for bringing to you such a fatuous request."

Campion remained staring at the pad in front of him. The ominous phrase danced before his eyes: "It is written in the ink." Suddenly he looked up.

"Where are you staying?"

"The Cosmopolitan. I'll be there for a week." He hesitated, then burst out, "If you think you can help me, for God's sake tell me."

Campion held out his hand.

"My dear chap, how can I promise anything?"

The other man would not be dismissed.

"Something has occurred to you. You know something."

"I don't know anything," Campion objected. "If I did, believe me, I'd have a great deal more to say. You must see I can't promise anything. But if it's any comfort to you, I can assure you that I shall spend the next day or so investigating a little mystery of my own which may conceivably have a bearing on your case. I can't say any more, truly, I can't say any more, can I?"

It took time to get rid of him but when at last the big man went down the staircase to the street, Campion stood by the window and watched until his visitor's long car moved quietly out of the cul-de-sac.

Some of the other man's passionate indignation had communicated itself to him and he, too, experienced a little of that helpless rage against the unknown. He went back to the desk and glanced once more at the pad.

"'He must have seen it all the time.'" Campion repeated the words softly. "I wonder..."

On the telephone Superintendent Oates was sympathetic but inclined to be heavily sarcastic.

"Oh yes, we'll do all your donkey work for you," he said cheerfully. "That's what the country pays us for. Anything you want to know, just ask the police. They like spadework. Live on it, in fact. All right, all right," his tone became plaintive as Campion protested, "I've said we'd do it, haven't I? Yes, we'll get out all the information you want about the party you've mentioned. But if you'd like my opinion, I think you've gone off your head."

Mr Campion thanked the Superintendent for his diagnosis and pointed out with dignity that he had not asked for it. He also presented his compliments to the Force and hoped it would get on with the job with more speed than was its custom.

As ever, when they both put down their telephones they were on the best of all possible terms.

Having put in motion the elementary machinery of an inquiry that he could but hope was not as forlorn as it appeared, Mr Albert Campion set to work on his own account. His first efforts were singularly unsuccessful. Lord Currier was out of town. Both he and his fiancée were guests in a house-party at Le Touquet. The date of their return was unknown.

Campion took the telephone receiver in his hand intending to call Miss Jennifer Pelham, but he thought better of it. The matter was delicate in the extreme and he shrank from the possibility of the snub direct.

Instead, in his quandary, he approached Lady Frinton.

That voluble old lady was delighted to hear his voice and said so at considerable length, but when at last he got in his request she was suddenly and uncharacteristically silent.

"The Pelham child?" she said at last, her tone dubious, "Phillida's youngest? The one with the red hair? *That* girl?"

Mr Campion was not to be distracted.

"The youngest Miss Pelham," he insisted patiently, "I want an introduction."

"Ye-es." Lady Frinton sounded hesitant. "You'd better come to see me," she said after a pause. "I hate telephones."

At the appointed hour Mr Campion presented himself at Lady Frinton's door in Knightsbridge and braced himself for an interview which promised to be exhausting.

When he was shown in to her Lady Frinton was sitting by the open window overlooking her small paved garden, and Campion saw immediately that she was prepared to be on her guard. His anxiety increased as she overwhelmed him with a flood of small talk which bid fair to be as inexhaustible as his patience, but after half an hour on the weather, the state of the country, her many religious beliefs and her ailing pets, he cornered her. His direct question pulled her up.

"Oh yes, that Pelham girl," she said, blinking at him. "Well, my dear, you know I'm a great friend of her mother and you know I couldn't abuse a confidence. I shouldn't bother with the child if I were you. She's very young."

Mr Campion leant back and folded his hands. He made a very personable figure lounging there, easily, in the needlework chair.

"I only want to meet her," he said plaintively.

Lady Frinton's shrewd blue eyes appraised him and he was relieved to see her smile.

"My dear, you really are charming," she said. "So old-world, too. I only wish I could help you, but I'm afraid you must wait. Young girls have these difficult spells but, thank goodness, they get over them."

Mr Campion's eyes flickered but his face registered nothing more intelligent than vague regret.

"What is it? The ballet or a footballer?" he inquired affably.

"Oh, nothing like that, the child's simply neurotic. I'm trying to persuade Phillida to take her to my yogi man. She has crying fits, ungovernable tempers, morbid desires for solitude and so on and so on."

Lady Frinton gave the information as though it had been dragged from her and then spread out her plump hands to indicate, no doubt, that she washed them of all responsibility.

"You must wait, my dear. Phillida says the girl won't see anybody. Just before the wedding, too. So unreasonable. Of course, it may be jealousy. These young people…"

She shrugged her shoulders and Campion laughed. The old lady bristled.

"Believe me, I'm not making mountains out of molehills. Why, the child actually wanted to throw up her part in the Jewel Pageant after her mother positively fought for a place for her, and we're all lending her our opals. We had quite a little scene the other night and poor Phillida simply had to put her foot down. The girl's impossible, Albert. She's spoiling her looks, too, the little idiot. If I'd behaved like that when I was young my mother would have taken a hairbrush to me."

Campion sat blinking at his hostess. He looked monumentally stupid.

"The Jewel Pageant?" he repeated. "Would that be the show at the Babylonian?"

"Well, of course it is." Lady Frinton gaped at him. "Dora is getting it up for one of those eternal charities." She spoke of her distinguished kinswoman, the Duchess of Stell, with tolerant amusement. "A host of young females are going to parade, each representing some jewel. The Pelham girl wasn't really eligible because she's still at school, but Phillida moved heaven and earth to get her in, and now the wretched creature has turned temperamental." She looked at her watch. "There's a rehearsal going on now. I expect there's been trouble over that. I am sorry for Phillida. When I was fifteen, I'd have given my ears to appear in public in a blaze of jewellery. Dora is lending the child her opal coronet and there's not another like it in England."

Campion took his leave. As he passed the sunburst clock with the garden face, he saw it was a quarter past five, and congratulated himself on a very instructive hour. Twenty-five minutes later he entered the ballroom of the Babylonian.

Her Grace, the Duchess of Stell, her hat on the back of her head and her broad face pink with exertion, nodded to him affably.

"Frightful!" she murmured confidentially, waving her program toward a group of forlorn young women on the platform at the far end of the room. "Look at them. We ought to have had professional models, but, of course, people won't lend their jewellery then, so what can one do?" Then she shrieked. "Come, girls, we'll go through that once more. Mary, Mary, my dear. You're diamonds, aren't you? Round the stage, come on then, all of you. Round again, slowly."

She hurried down the room and Campion drifted toward the

group of privileged onlookers, program girls and other assistants who stood about on the polished floor.

Meanwhile, the awkward squad of granddaughters and nieces of the flower of England's nobility wriggled and did their inadequate best.

Mr Campion took up position directly behind the undieted mamas and so was able to observe the stage without much danger of being himself observed. He located Jennifer Pelham and was startled to see the change in her. She wore green still, but her face was sharp and weary, and her eyes hunted. As he watched he was aware that there was in her a certain conscious clumsiness. She moved with deliberate awkwardness and her mistakes were so absurd that they were entirely unconvincing. Campion was puzzled by her movements until the moment when she stumbled and collapsed. Then the explanation for her behaviour came to him with the force of a minor revelation.

For years the Duchess had approved of Mr Campion. In the next few moments he earned her undying gratitude. No one could have behaved with greater tact and despatch, no one could have been more helpful than Albert Campion. He swept through the chattering throng, gathered up the limp Miss Pelham and, explaining that his car was in the courtyard, declared his intention of taking her home immediately. Jennifer lay gracefully in his arms, her eyes determinedly shut. Only once did she open them, and that was when the Duchess, clucking over her like a distressed Wyandotte, murmured something about tomorrow's performance. At that moment Jennifer's heavy lids flickered wide.

"I can't," she murmured, "I'm so sorry. Somebody else," then she relapsed against Mr Campion's lapel.

Her Grace sighed.

"It'll have to be the Carter girl," she said. "After all, opals are large and vague. It won't really matter. Still, I am sorry. Take the poor child home, Albert. Her colour's still good so it can't be anything very serious. Tell Phillida I'll phone this evening. I can't thank you enough, Albert. You are a comforting boy. Take her along."

Mr Campion remained the soul of knight errantry until he had reached the Lagonda and packed his fainting burden into the front seat. His efficiency was remarkable. He stove off the anxious and well-meaning guests at the rehearsal and made his rescue from collapse to car in a little under seven minutes.

As he swung the grey automobile out into the traffic his manner underwent a change.

"Sit up!" he said curtly. "Doubtless you have your own reasons for this histrionic display but there's no need to get a crick in the back of your neck. You look rather silly, too."

The fainting girl blushed, and a smile curved the corners of Campion's wide mouth as he glanced at her.

"Too difficult, my child," he said. "If you must dissemble, choose a violent internal pain or acute rheumatism of the knee joint. The swoon is too exacting. Even the greatest of tragediennes, Eleanora Duse, couldn't fool a Boy Scout at close quarters."

He paused abruptly. Jennifer's fiery colour had disappeared. A single tear, very large and round, squeezed beneath her left eyelid and bumped down the steep curves of her face. Mr Campion felt himself a cad and had the grace to say so.

"What's up?" he inquired.

"N-n-nothing. I'm all right. Put me in a taxi, if you like." She spoke humbly.

The Lagonda was caught in a traffic-jam. He braked and sat regarding her.

"Do you remember me?" he asked.

For a moment she stared at him, then her eyes grew wide and she fumbled at the door-catch beside her. Mr Campion felt unreasonably angry.

"Look out," he said sharply. "At least let me put you down on the pavement. If you get out that side, you'll walk into a bus."

She turned slowly and stared at him again.

"I don't care," she said and the intensity in the young voice was terrible.

At that moment the stream of traffic moved sluggishly forward and the Lagonda crawled on in the procession. Campion did not look at Jennifer and when he spoke again his tone was serious but comfortingly calm.

"Look here," he said, "I don't want to butt into your affairs but I'm not quite the ape I look, and I might conceivably be able to lend a useful hand. You're terrified, aren't you?"

He felt her shiver at his side.

"A bit," she admitted huskily.

"I ask you again; what's up?"

"I can't tell you."

"You daren't; that's it, isn't it?"

"Yes — no — I don't know. Take me home, please."

Campion nodded his regretful acquiescence.

"All right. Forgive me. We turn here, don't we?"

She sat very still and stiff until they reached Clarges Street, but as the car slid to a standstill she plucked at his sleeve, a frightened little gesture that was oddly disarming.

"Don't please tell anyone I didn't really faint," she said, her extreme alarm counteracting the childish naïveté of the words. "Don't tell anyone. I can't explain, but it's terribly important. You see, I just had to get out of wearing all that jewellery and yet I've got to go to the Dover House Ball the day after tomorrow. Promise, please, promise."

He looked at her squarely.

"You can rely on me," he said, "but, if I were you, I'd risk it and tell me the whole yarn. I can usually fix these things. It's a sort of hobby of mine."

The younger Miss Pelham caught her breath.

"I can't," she said, "not *you*. Not *you*, especially *not* you."

This emphatic statement was so unexpected that Mr Campion

blinked in astonishment. Jennifer, seizing her opportunity, fled into the house as if all the furies were behind her.

Mr Campion drove slowly and thoughtfully to Scotland Yard.

Superintendent Oates sat behind his square desk and regarded his visitor with a mixture of curiosity and grudging admiration.

"Where have you been all the day?" he demanded. "I've been looking for you everywhere. How do you do it? Second sight or just plain guesswork?"

Campion raised his eyebrows.

"Turned up anything?" he inquired.

"Plenty; and Mr Allen has been in here with a cable from his American agent. There's a chance you may be right. Some people get all the luck."

The Superintendent, a spare, grey man with the enthusiasm of a boy, rubbed his hands cheerfully.

"Well," he said, "we've looked up the man you suggested, and the dates are okay. He was in New York at the right time and he certainly visited the same houses as poor Mrs Allen. Of course, there's no proof but it's interesting, to say the least of it. Then this cable this afternoon takes us a step further. Some of her jewellery has been traced and by sheer good luck the purchaser took the numbers of the notes with which he paid her for it. And now a goodly parcel of these notes has turned up in a Brooklyn bank. The bank officials think they may be able to furnish a description of the man who deposited the notes. It's pretty slender, but it's better than nothing. Waldo Allen is trying to persuade us to hold your man, this suspect of yours, for inquiries when we get the full dope from New York. I must say I don't like it. Better to catch a chap like him actually at work."

Campion sat down.

"Can I talk unofficially?" he asked quietly.

Oates stared at him and, impressed by his manner, checked the flippancy which was close to his lips.

"Of course," he said. "Are you on to something? What's on your mind?"

Mr Campion put his cards on the table while the Superintendent listened with his head on one side, terrier fashion.

"You say we must keep this girl out of it?" Oates said at last. "Well, if it's blackmail that's quite possible. It's an incredible story. I don't see his game, not yet, not quite. A young married woman with her own bank account is one thing, but a fifteen-year-old could only give him chicken-feed, surely?"

Mr Campion looked lazily at the policeman.

"This fifteen-year-old was about to be entrusted with many thousands of pounds' worth of opals," he murmured. "She was to wear them all the evening. The prospect so frightened her that she threw up her part in this pageant. It was rather an important treat to miss for a kid of that age."

Oates was silent for a moment.

"It has been done," he admitted at last. "I don't like it, Campion, I don't like it at all, but still, let's keep our sense of proportion." He had another thought. "What could a child of that age have to hide?"

"That I can't possibly imagine." Campion spoke gravely, his pale eyes puzzled. He could not shake from his mind Jennifer's final remark to him.

The Superintendent cut through his thoughts.

"Since you're so keen on it, we might start an investigation without committing ourselves. I don't mind telling you we've had a tip from up above to do everything we can for Mr Allen. What do you suggest?"

"A word with the organisers of the Dover House Ball," said Mr Campion promptly. "Then a couple of your men, me, and you yourself, if you feel like it — four of us in all. What do you say?"

"It's crazy," said the Superintendent. "You could be on to entirely the wrong man."

"That's a possibility, but if I read aright one of Allen's two clues, then I'm not. The day after tomorrow?"

Oates sighed. "All right. I'll get out my boiled shirt and come with you. But I warn you, if you get me into a stiff collar for nothing..."

He left the threat dangling in air, but Mr Campion appeared not to be listening.

There were, in fact, five of them keeping vigil in a small enclosure some forty-eight hours later. Superintendent Oates, Mr Campion, two young officers from the Mayfair squad and Waldo Allen who had insisted on accompanying them. Just outside their prison the thick black velvet curtains of a tent hung motionless. Around them the music and chatter of one of the greatest balls of the summer season eddied and swirled. The night was hot, there was scarcely enough room for the five men in the space where they hid, and they were close to smothering.

Superintendent Oates stood like a rock, his keen ears strained and one hand resting upon the sleeve of the American. From not far away they heard the sound of someone striking a match. This was the pre-arranged signal which told them that the detective on duty at the ball had seen Jennifer Pelham enter the fortune teller's booth. The five men stiffened.

For a moment all was quiet on the other side of the curtain, then a young voice said huskily: "I'm here."

Cagliostro the Second did not reply immediately and Campion guessed that he had gone to the opening of the tent to see if there were anyone about. Campion knew that the room outside was deserted for he had arranged that in advance. After a pause he heard the fortune teller's voice, slow and very cold.

"You failed."

"I couldn't go. I was ill. Honestly, I was ill. I fainted at rehearsal and they had to send me home."

The girl's voice was barely audible. Oates felt the American stir at his side and grasped his sleeve all the more firmly. Cagliostro spoke again.

"I am growing angry with you." The quiet voice on the other side of the curtain had a menacing quality out of all proportion to the words.

"I gave you your opportunity. You had but to walk to a window and drop the jewellery out. In ten minutes you could have given the alarm. I asked you for nothing impossible. I was kind enough to show you a way to settle your debt. Now I shall not help you any further. You must pay me, Miss Pelham."

"I can't, I tell you, I can't!" Jennifer was on the edge of hysteria. "I've given you every penny I've got. Let that be enough. Give me back my letters. You got them by a trick."

"Not at all. You gave them to me."

"I just put them in an envelope for you to put under your crystal. I didn't know you were going to give me back a different envelope with a piece of newspaper in it. Give me the letters, please. They're not mine."

Cagliostro laughed. "If they were yours, they'd hardly be so interesting," he said. "You haven't even read them, have you? If you had, my dear, I think you'd be more obliging. I shall be at the Courtney reception on the twenty-third. Get yourself invited. Come in to see me in the ordinary way and bring me something else to put in an envelope under the crystal — this time two hundred and fifty pounds in one-pound notes. It's not a large sum; I choose it because I think you can raise that much. When I see the money then I'll return your dangerous letters!"

"I can't."

No sooner did he hear the girl's despairing exclamation than Waldo Allen charged, brushing aside the Superintendent's attempt to restrain him as if it had never been made.

It was not an edifying scene and afterward the organisers of the ball, who had co-operated with the police against their better judgment, had a good deal to say on the subject.

Oates maintained his dignity and insisted that the commotion had been restricted to the tent and to the room which held the tent.

As ever, Mr Campion had shown himself capable of calm in an emergency. He it was who realised that the first objective must be to prevent murder.

Waldo Allen was at last dragged away from the gasping creature who had called himself a psychometrist.

Cagliostro was unceremoniously hustled into a waiting police car.

Quietly, Mr Campion climbed the stairs to the room where the dismantled tent lay, a pool of inky wreckage on the parqueted floor. The detectives on duty stood woodenly by the closed doors into the ballroom.

It was some moments before Campion saw Miss Pelham curled up in the corner of a couch, her head in her arms.

He sat down beside her and solemnly proffered his handkerchief. "Cheer up, old lady," he murmured. "The worst is over. The tooth is out."

She raised a tear-stained face to his.

"You don't understand," she whispered. "Now they'll find the letters."

Campion sat up. "Of course," he said. "Bless me, whose were they? Your sister's?"

She gulped, and the tears dried from her eyes like a startled child's. "How did you know?"

Realising that to confess to the gift of divination is a weakness, Mr Campion did not reply directly.

"Don't you think that it might help if you explained it all in your own words? You stole the letters in the first place; I saw you, remember. We'll skate over that. I take it you had a natural sisterly anxiety to discover the sort of man your Roberta was marrying, and you thought our unpleasant pal Cagliostro was the man to read the oracle. Is that right?"

She nodded miserably. "I'm a sentimental, theatrical little ass," she said with sudden frankness, adding grimly, "I mean, I used to be. I'm also rather mad; careless and muddle-headed, you know. The idea came to me suddenly and I knew Roberta kept her private letters in that bureau. I just rushed off to get them, meaning to put them back, of course, as soon as I'd heard the reading from the fortune teller. You startled me, and I took the first package of letters that came to hand. I didn't even look at them. I just tore downstairs and then hung about until I could slip into the tent. I had some sort of idiotic idea I was looking after Roberta, don't you see, and then this went and happened."

Mr Campion was sympathetic. "They weren't from our Thomas?" he said. "Whose were they? D'you know?"

The younger Miss Pelham started to weep again. "Bobby Fellowes, I think," she said. "They had a sort of silly affair last year. He's frightfully young, and Roberta rather passed him on to me. He brought me here tonight, as a matter of fact. Now it will all come out, Thomas will break off his engagement and Roberta will break her heart. Bobby will be livid, too. I can't bear it! I didn't know anything had happened until I opened the envelope. I thought it was the same one that I'd sealed the package in. But when I did open it, I saw it wasn't. I simply thought there'd been a mistake and I went back to Cagliostro. He was frightfully serious. He said the letters showed Roberta's infidelity and he suggested I buy them back. I gave him all the money I had but it wasn't enough. You know the rest."

Mr Campion's pleasant face was grim. "Yes, well," he said. "I shouldn't worry any more. I'll get Master Fellowes' letters back for you, that I promise. Meanwhile, if it's any comfort to you, let me tell you that I've known Thomas since he was four feet high, and if you think any youthful endearments from your young pal Bobby would take his mind off your sister, then, my child, you're insane."

Jennifer breathed deeply. "Oh, I wasn't afraid of Thomas," she said, "but have you heard of Uncle John?"

Mr Campion's eyes were opened. "Heaven forgive me!" he said piously. "I actually forgot Uncle John. You poor kid! Of course, you were alarmed. Well, look here, you go home and go to bed and I'll deliver the documents in a plain van tomorrow morning. That's a bet. Any good?"

When Miss Pelham's powers of expressing her gratitude were partially exhausted a faintly puzzled expression crept into her eyes. "Why did *you* take so much trouble over it all?" she demanded.

Campion regarded her seriously. "Who is Sylvia?" he said. "I think she must have been a little girl very like you."

Later that night the Superintendent sat in Mr Campion's Piccadilly flat and sipped a long drink to which he felt he was justly entitled.

"Yes, well, we've got him," he said. "The nerve of the fellow! There was nothing in those letters, Campion, nothing at all. I looked at them. Boy Scout stuff. Yet he got two hundred quid out of the kid. What I don't see is how he did it. He swapped envelopes about, that I see, but how did he hit on the right ones to keep? I mean, he could well have picked on some woman who'd simply raise Cain at the first sign of any monkey business."

Campion leant back in his chair. "My dear chap," he said, "that's where he was so clever. He picked his victims, not his evidence. Whenever a helpless-looking little girl gave him a package that felt like a bundle of love-letters he gave her back a dummy envelope and then examined what he had. If he thought they were interesting he worked his insufferable racket. If they weren't, he handed them back with an apology and some convincing story about a mistake."

"But these letters weren't what you call interesting," Oates objected. "Far from it."

"I don't know. They weren't the girl's own, you see, and they weren't from the sister's distinguished fiancé with the budding career in the Diplomatic and the irascible Uncle John. Cagliostro heard all the gossip, remember. All he had to do was to find out if Jennifer had read them. When he found she had not, all was plain sailing."

"Skunk!" said Oates. "Allen called him that and it suits him. We'll put him away all right, without publicity. I say, Campion, forgive a professional question, but what put you on to him?"

Campion frowned. "'It is written in the ink,'" he quoted. "D'you remember that?"

"Yes, I do. Mrs Allen said it before she committed suicide, didn't she? It still doesn't convey anything to me."

"Nor me at first," admitted Campion modestly. "But the story of the blackmailed innocent reminded me of Jennifer, and Jennifer reminded me of that damned fortune teller, so I put two and two together."

"I'll buy it," said the Superintendent.

"It's ridiculously simple. When first I looked into the tent, I saw a crystal. A fortune teller of that kind doesn't have a crystal as a rule. He simply holds the envelope, or whatever it is, and goes into a trance. That was just a little oddity that set me thinking, and from crystals, naturally, I went on to ink. In India the fakirs look into a pool of ink instead of a crystal, you know."

"I didn't. Still, go on."

Campion sighed. "You're an impossible person to have to explain thought-processes to," he said. "But if those last words had been 'it is written in the crystal' you'd have automatically thought of fortune tellers, wouldn't you? Well, then, the ink is sometimes synonymous with the crystal, and when there's a terrified young girl in each situation, well, it sets you wondering. That's all."

Oates laughed explosively.

"In fact, you guessed it. You picked a winning horse with a pin," he said. "My word, Campion, you're lucky! There was no brains in it at all."

Mr Campion looked hurt. There are times when he feels it is his destiny to be underestimated by his friends.

SWEET AND LOW

I t's a nice day."

"Beautiful."

"Been nice all this week."

"Very."

"Is that an over-reach on your off foreleg?"

"No. He cut it on a piece of filthy tin in your long meadow. It's practically healed."

"Oh, sorry. About the tin, I mean. It's a nice day."

"Beautiful. I'm late for lunch. Goodbye."

Susan turned Taffy abruptly and trotted off smartly down the lower road, and that was that.

She did not look back at the young man who was so long that he seemed to fit into his small open car with difficulty but was sufficiently feminine to hope that he noticed how flat her shoulders were under her new brown hacking coat.

When she was certain she had heard the car turn the corner on to the Tipton road she relaxed considerably and permitted Taffy to drop into the leisurely trot he liked best.

Susan was resolutely against heart-searching. Her attitude toward Phil Biringstone was, she reflected, cold, impersonal and a trifle worldly. He could break his neck for all she cared. No; perhaps not actually his neck, but his leg or an arm. Or anyway he could shake himself up a bit and lose some of his wretched superiority. Courage like his was all very well in Susan's opinion. If a man has been born in the saddle — well, practically so — it's perfectly natural for him to feel more at home on a horse than on his own two enormous feet. But even if he is so incredibly brave and does take jumps in the hunting field that make one go cold inside and does ride a notoriously nappy six-year-old to victory in the point-to-point, leaving the Army struggling like bogged goats at the seventh fence, is there any reason why he should go all condescending to a girl on a very good pony when he finds her scrambling through a patch of furze in an undignified attempt to avoid a three-foot hedge with a ditch on the other side?

The incident had taken place at the final meet of the season. Susan had been getting on very nicely, with Taffy nosing his way like a pointer among the furze and cautiously feeling every step with his little round hooves before he trusted their combined weight on the spongy clay, when Phil Birlingstone had left the hunt to come after her and, with a face as scarlet as his coat, had bellowed ungallantly:

"Look out! Look out, you little idiot! There's a mass of rabbit-holes in there. You'll kill yourself or your poor beast."

That in itself had been insulting enough. But when Geraldine Partington-Drew had joined him on her magnificent bay ("only eight-fifty, my dear. They positively gave her to me because I could manage her") Susan had tasted mud. They sat towering over her on their great mounts and actually laughed — or at least Geraldine had laughed. Phil had merely scowled until Susan backed the protesting Taffy into the open meadow again. Then Geraldine had ridden off, calling to Phil to follow her, and actually, of course, to make them watch her take the jump as cleanly and clearly as a cat.

Phil had followed her, but not before he had added the final

straw. Susan blushed with righteous rage whenever she remembered his words, and that meant she blushed on an average twice
a day.

"I'll go first," he had said. "You won't want me to stand and
watch you, will you?"

Susan glowered when she remembered it. The impudence, the
conceit, the insufferable superiority of the man was incredible.

She dug her heels into Taffy's fat sides and startled that old
gentleman into a canter to relieve her feelings.

When they were both in peace and comfort again her indignation settled into calm contempt once more.

Geraldine would marry Phil eventually; everybody saw that
coming. In her more worldly moments (and when one is twenty-
one can feel worldly with the assurance that one knows what one
is about) Susan was inclined to approve of the match. They were
both wealthy, Phil had a title, and Geraldine had thousands and
thousands of pounds to make up for a father like Partington-
Drew, they were both horse-crazy, both magnificent riders, both
utterly fearless and, even if Geraldine had reached the advanced
age of twenty-nine and did look a little like her own mare, especially about the nose, she had heaps of money for clothes and
things and often appeared remarkably handsome in the saddle.

When she was very frank with herself Susan considered that
her own dislike of Miss Partington-Drew was perfectly natural
and excusable. In a way it was jealousy. Susan was prepared to
admit that and even to condone it.

Before the Partington-Drews had bought the Old Rectory and
turned that white elephant of the Ecclesiastical Commissioners
into a glittering palace of hot-water taps, central heating and
marble baths, Susan and Taffy had been the pets of the village and
the white hope of the horse-loving farmers round about.

Then it had been only natural for the daughter of Captain
Mavis, RN of the Grange, and now a hard-working kennel maid
to the local vet, to trot in and out of the stable yard at the hall

whenever Taffy's minor ailments required the attentions of Lady Birlingstone's elderly groom, the faithful and beloved Henry Branch, who had patently been a horse himself in some previous incarnation, so surely did he divine the slightest equine trouble.

When Phil had returned from abroad to take up his duties as head of the house on his father's death his eye had quite naturally rested with interest upon the trim little figure on the chestnut pony. There was nothing in that. Most eyes rested on Susan with interest. She was so used to it that it had become ordinary.

They had got on very well together and Phil had seemed to share the village's interest in her riding. He was about to acquire a couple of hunters and old Lady Birlingstone, who was the sweetest, silliest old darling in Debrett, had thought of asking her son-in-law, Tony March, who knew about thoroughbreds and had a very fine stable of his own away in the north of the county, if he could not pick up a little blood mare which Susan might care to ride sometimes.

At this period there were discreet bets in the Queen's Head on the chances of a popular wedding at Easter in the following year and everything had looked very exciting for the first time in Susan's young life, when, only three months after Phil's return home, the Partington-Drews had arrived and with them Geraldine.

Geraldine had not achieved her present position immediately, but it had not taken her long, for she treated men as she treated horses; that is to say, with a firm, light hand and indomitable will and tremendous personal courage.

The village was inclined to jeer at her at first but her stable of four expensive hunters and a prize-winning show jumper had impressed it in spite of itself, and when she had won the Ladies' Race in three out of the four adjacent point-to-points and had hinted that she was taking the jumper to the County's Royal Show it sighed and capitulated.

Old Henry Branch alone was faithful. When he had first set

eyes on Susan and Taffy, he had described the ensemble as "the prettiest sight I ever see" and had remained obstinately of that opinion ever since.

A little question concerning the confusion of "sprain" and "far-sie" had settled him with Geraldine forever. Geraldine had disdained his advice and sent for the vet and had not apologised on finding herself in the wrong. From that time forward he admitted Geraldine could ride but considered her "a proper bouncy lady."

Of late Mr Branch had been worried. He had set his heart on Miss Susan coming to be the lady of the hall and at one time had been prepared to bet on the eventuality at the rate of three pints to one, but, as the days passed, and Miss Geraldine displayed more ingenuity in devising excuses for absorbing all Sir Phil's spare time than Branch had thought to exist in the whole plaguey world of women put together, his spirits sank.

Miss Susan was evidently not going to make a fight for it and Branch, while respecting her maidenly restraint, regretted the ruthless determination of her rival. Of Sir Phil himself, since he was his employer, he kept his thoughts to himself.

There were other people besides Branch who were appalled by the seemingly inevitable trend of events and they were not so discreet.

Old Lady Birlingstone opened her heart to her daughter Jean.

"It's not that I mind the girl Geraldine," she said pathetically, rubbing her ear with her gardening glove. "She's quite a nice crea-ture, no doubt, even if she is so masterful and has such a distressing voice. But no woman likes to see her son roped like a — like a..."

"Steer, Mother," said Jean, who was practical and not unmas-terful herself.

"Steer is it?" repeated Lady Birlingstone vaguely. "Well, anyway, I don't like to see him *rushed*. He's slow. His father was. Susan is so *pretty*, Jean. I thought she was beginning to care for him. He had a snapshot of her on Taffy. I found it in a suit I sent to the jumble sale. I took it out, of course. Villagers do jump to conclusions so quickly. I put the snapshot on Phil's dressing table, as a little hint, you know, but the next morning it was in the grate all torn up. I was so sorry."

"Is he now carting around a snap of the acquisitive Geraldine?" inquired the forthright Jean, standing with her hands in her jodhpur pockets.

"Oh, no. She gave him a big photograph." Lady Birlingstone rubbed the mud off her ear with her handkerchief and looked worried. "He can't carry that about. It's meant to be framed. He's put it in his shirt drawer, right at the bottom. I don't know if he's hiding it from us or from himself. She'll get him, Jean, I know it. I've seen it happen over and over again. It's not that men are exactly weak, but they are lazy, and they don't like to be rude, and what with one thing and another they get pushed this way and that and are hustled and bothered until they can't see any way out of the difficulty except to...to..."

"Gather up their heels and pop over the fence," supplemented Jean thoughtfully. "I know. I've seen Geraldine do that in the hunting field. Well, darling, we must see what can be done. I'll talk to Tony."

Talking to Tony was Jean's favourite expedient when in doubt and Lady Birlingstone gave her blessing brightly.

"I wish you would, dear," she said. She had great faith in her son-in-law.

Tony March was not altogether unworthy of his mother-in-law's trust. At least he was always prepared to *do* something, and, if his ideas were occasionally a trifle school-boyish, he certainly carried them out with devotion and a strict attention to detail. Aided by his enthusiastic young wife, he gave the matter his earnest attention.

Meanwhile, Susan went on her proud and worldly way mercifully unconscious of the forces gathering to her assistance.

She did not hear about Sweet and Low until Geraldine met her in the dentist's waiting room nearly a month after Lady Birlingstone's appeal to her married daughter.

It was not the best time to talk horses to anyone, but Geraldine was never tactful.

"Hello," she said as Susan came in, treading resolutely, her mind on local anaesthetics. "I haven't seen you for years. What have you been doing? Hiding?"

"No," said Susan, trying not to be pleased that Miss Partington-Drew still looked very raw about the nose and cheekbones although hunting was long-since over, "just living."

"I know." Geraldine had a loud, resonant voice and a tendency to accentuate the operative word. "My dear, one does nothing, absolutely nothing, except ride. I don't see a soul save Phil."

Susan winced and could have kicked herself. She had an insane temptation to say, "Phil who?" but, since Geraldine could not be expected to be quite obtuse, she saved her face in time.

"I'm taking Bitter Aloes, my mare, to Minstree Show on the nineteenth," said Geraldine, who was apparently as nonchalant before the dentist's chair as she was in the hunting field. "It's a first-class rehearsal. All the intelligent people use it. There are some nice Irish horses coming over."

Susan, who had ridden in the Pony class at the Minstree Show until she had been superannuated at the age of fourteen, nodded wisely.

"The jumping there's pretty hot, nearly up to the Royal standard," she murmured.

Miss Partington-Drew laughed.

"Still, I think we may pull it off," she said, and was doubly irritating because she was probably perfectly right. "Bitter Aloes is very good, you know. Of course I haven't the faintest idea what Phil has up his sleeve."

Susan pricked up her ears. It was distressing to hear news from the hall in this roundabout way. In the old days a new horse would have called forth a celebration at which her presence would have been indispensable.

Geraldine was sufficiently feminine to sense a hit.

"Didn't you know?" she said. "I thought everyone heard everything in villages. Tony March has bought a new show jumper, Sweet and Low. They say he's marvellous. Phil is to ride him at Minstree and as far as I can hear we shall fight it out between us. It ought to be tremendous fun. Phil is going to stay with the Marchs at Benley. Their place is only six or seven miles from Minstree."

"I know," said Susan, who had known the house since childhood. "I shall be there," she added primly.

"Will you? What with? Your little pony?" Geraldine did not exactly sneer, Susan had to admit that, but she did laugh a little and Susan blushed.

"Yes," she said. "My little cousin rides him in the Under Fourteen Hands."

"How amusing! How are you getting him there? I shall box Bitter Aloes, of course, or I'd lend you mine."

"I always stay at my aunt's at Finchingtree and hack the three miles over." For all her sophistication Susan could have wept.

"How amusing!" said Geraldine again and Susan was saved from making a bitter and revealing reply by the beaming nurse who came to summon her to the torture chamber.

For practically the first time in her life she found the ghoulish leer of old Mr Fortnum almost welcome, but as she leant back in the chair, she caught a glimpse of the Partington-Drew Rolls-Royce parked in the High Street outside and there was rage in her heart. Things had come to a pretty pass if a girl couldn't go to the dentist's in peace.

On the morning of the Minstree Show Tony March sat on the end of his wife's bed, his round, ingenuous face wearing an expression of secret guile. He was both happy and excited, but, being a comparatively practical man, was carefully going over his tactics for the day with his second-in-command.

"It all depends on you, old dear," he said, regarding his wife fondly. "You must put up a good show or he'll smell a rat, and that would be absolutely fatal. I rather thought he was getting wind of something fishy last night."

"Last night?" protested Jean. "But he couldn't! He simply couldn't. I mean, we haven't done anything yet."

Tony shook his round head.

"Phil's a funny chap," he announced. "As brave as a lion, knows all there is to know about horses, but one disadvantage; he doesn't talk. It's very hard to get out of him what's on his mind."

"If he hasn't said anything, I don't see how you can possibly suppose he's noticed something fishy," declared Jean cheerfully.

"Oh, but he has," Tony persisted. "He has spoken. It was just before we came up to bed last night. We were having a drink when he suddenly put down his glass and made a very extraordinary remark. He said, 'That's a funny horse you've got, old boy.'"

"Yes, and then what?"

"Oh, he didn't say any more, naturally." Tony seemed surprised that she should have expected it. "I said, 'Really?' or 'Do you think so?' or 'Not at all,' something vague like that, and we left it and went to bed. Still, I thought it off he should have said so much. I wouldn't have things go wrong for anything."

Jean sniffed and stretched her long arms over her head.

"I shouldn't worry about *Phil*," she said. "When I saw he'd brought Branch over yesterday I felt a bit nervous. Branch is an entirely different proposition. Still, he hasn't seen the brute at work and after all Sweet and Low can jump."

"Oh, yes," said Tony earnestly, "he can jump. Jump! Oh, lord, yes! He can jump. Gosh! Yes. Jump?"

He went on murmuring to himself on the same theme for some time. Jean giggled.

"Phil was right," she said. "He is a funny horse."

There was a moment of silence between the two conspirators before Tony left the initial danger-point and went on to the next.

"I'll just run through it once more," he began cheerfully. "Keep your mind on it, sweetheart. First, we get old Branch off with the horse. Then we fool about and manage to be very late starting. Finally, when we're actually on the road, you fall ill, and we stop near a pub. You make a frightful fuss and we both have to stay with you or rush off to get a doctor or something. Then Phil says, 'What about the show?' and I say, 'Forget the show! Think of my wife...'"

Jean frowned. "Don't overdo that bit," she murmured. "I mean, don't declaim it, or anything."

Tony was hurt. "You leave it to me," he said. "I'll sound convincing. After a bit I'll have an idea. I'll phone the ground, get hold of Branch and tell him to ask Miss Partington-Drew if she'll take Sweet and Low round as a special favour to Sir Philip. She'll leap at the invitation. Meanwhile, you'll start recovering and we'll go on, arriving at Minstree just after Geraldine has been round on Sweet and Low. Phil will trot up, smiling, and ask her how she got on and that will be definitely that."

"Why?" Jean's question was not very innocent, but Tony was gulled by it.

"Don't be silly, sweetheart," he protested wearily. "We've gone over this again and again. Geraldine will give Phil one long eloquent glance and never speak to him again. He will be furious at her injustice and the rebound will send him scuttling off to young Susan. This is the whole point of the scheme. Hang it, you thought of quite half of it yourself."

"I know, but I'm getting nervous." Jean shivered happily. "Geraldine is very determined, darling. She may just stick her toes in and cling to him."

Tony sighed. He hated any objections when he was making plans.

"My dearest child," he expostulated, "think of that show ring! Think of the crowd who will be there. There will be absolutely everyone Geraldine's ever met or hopes to meet. They've all heard her talk about herself. She won't cling to Phil. We shall have to get him away before she beats him up."

Jean lay back among the pillows.

"She may win on Sweet and Low," she murmured.

Tony's bucolic face became bland and childlike.

"If she rides as well as she thinks she does, she will," he said sweetly. "That's the beauty of the whole idea. It's so fair."

The Machiavellian activities of young Mr and Mrs March met with singular success, at least in their earlier stages.

Jean's seizure in the car just outside the Farrowfield Plough Inn was so realistic that even her husband, who was expecting it, was temporarily deceived and, so far, forgot his role as to pat her shoulder with an anxious if somewhat violent hand and to demand helplessly if she couldn't pull herself together until they reached the town.

Jean's natural indignation at this lack of support almost wrecked the project at the outset, but it was Phil himself who unwittingly saved the situation by exhibiting a wholly unsuspected solicitude for his sister.

It was Phil who saw her safely ensconced in the private room at the back of The Plough, Phil who conferred with the startled landlady, not unnaturally bewildered by the astonishing assortment of symptoms developed by the mendacious Jean, Phil who gallantly declared the show was of no importance, and Phil who sat chafing his sister's hand with doglike devotion and incompetence.

Since there was nothing left for the arch-conspirator to do but to get on with his conspiracy, Tony rang up the show ground, got hold of Branch, and gave the message he had so carefully rehearsed.

Until this point, the disgraceful machinations of Mr and Mrs

March had met with more success than they deserved. Phil had played into their hands with a stupidity and a lack of penetration unworthy of him and no doctor had yet arrived to regard Jean with a cold professional eye.

It is hardly conceivable that their well-meaning but impractical efforts could have resulted in anything approaching the object they desired had they been allowed to take their course uninterrupted, but as it happened not Fate, but an equally unaccountable deity, stepped in to defeat them. The spoke in the wheel was the soft human heart of Henry Branch.

As the old groom came back from the Committee's office, whence he had been summoned to the telephone to receive Tony's message, he observed a trim little figure in spotless kit standing somewhat forlornly by a resplendent pony. Susan attended to her own tack and her own grooming and Taffy did her credit. The green rosette which he wore as third prize-winner in his class suited him admirably.

Branch admired them both and, as his eye lighted on Susan's yellow head and dejected expression, a rebellious and unfortunate thought entered his mind.

Miss Geraldine Partington-Drew could ride, but so could Miss Susan. Seemingly Sir Phil had lost sight of that. Branch considered the big roan waiting in his box. He had never seen Sweet and Low at his work, but he had heard Mr Tony's glowing accounts of him and he had seen the high quarter-bone which meant the animal could jump. "You'll never get a bad goose-backed horse" was Branch's favourite aphorism and he had taken to Sweet and Low from the first. He liked his full, intelligent eyes, his pricked ears and the friendly, almost confidential way he hummered at him. In Branch's opinion Sweet and Low was a kind horse. If he had not been so sure of that he would never have thought of using his proverbial deafness and notorious distrust of telephones as an excuse for what was, in reality, sheer disobedience.

A little further along the paddock behind the double row of

cars round the ring he saw Miss Geraldine on Bitter Aloes. She was ready early and was sitting, proud and supremely confident, waiting for her own opportunity to shine.

Branch disliked her. He disliked the way she shouted at her grooms, he disliked her father's Rolls-Royce, he thought her mare too good for her and he dreaded the day when she should bring back Sir Phil from church on a halter.

He glanced at Susan again, and, in his mind's eye, saw her, flushed and triumphant, finishing a clean round on the goose-backed roan.

"I'm growing remarkable deaf," he observed to a total stranger who was passing him and set out with a happy grin on his tight-skinned face to interview Susan.

Susan heard the message with astonishment and an unexpected thrill which she attributed quite erroneously to her interest in show jumping generally. She had put in many extra hours' evening work to get this time off to attend the show and now was on the point of regretting coming. Everywhere she looked she seemed to see Geraldine. Now here was Branch with a wonderful request from Phil. He wanted her to ride the horse that he himself had been going to ride.

"Sir Phil's compliments, and would you do him the very great favour of taking Sweet and Low over the jumps. Those were his words, Miss."

Branch thought it best to omit Tony's presence on the telephone for the sake of clarity.

"He's held up hisself on the road."

"He's not hurt?" Susan blushed at her own anxiety and felt annoyed.

"No, no, Miss. It's Mrs Jean. She's been took faint."

"Jean faint? How extraordinary!"

Afterward Susan realised that she should have suspected the whole beastly business from that one illogical and unlikely circumstance, but at the time she was excited. She thought Phil was a supercilious and conceited oaf, but she was glad to know that even he recognised her riding was good, and she was amused to note that he still remembered her name even if he hadn't spoken to her for a couple of months. The chance of challenging Geraldine on her own ground was inviting, also.

"Come and see the horse, Miss," Branch persisted, anxious to get her in the saddle before his conscience got him down.

When Sweet and Low stepped daintily out of his box and he and Susan saw each other for the first time it is possible that they both laughed. Susan laughed openly because a strawberry roan with a white diamond over one eye is a comic spectacle, and Sweet and Low laughed secretly for deep and private reasons of his own.

Branch swept back the rug and displayed the jumping bone and for some minutes he and the lady who was so very specially his choice discussed points.

"He's got a mind of his own," said Branch at last when the air had ceased to buzz with technicalities. "Powerful lot of character in those ears."

Sweet and Low took Susan's hat off and stood holding it foolishly in his soft muzzle. Susan's heart was touched.

"He's a darling, Branch," she said laughing. "A darling. Not a bit nappy either."

"Nappy?" Branch laid a hand on the sleek withers. "He don't know the meaning of the word. I'd let a baby crawl round his feet."

When Susan slid into the saddle and gathered up her reins, she felt supremely happy.

Sweet and Low had the motion of an angel. His clownish face was more than offset by the magnificent dignity of his carriage and he seemed to like her hands for he did not fidget with her. When she turned him away from the crowds and down to the long meadow behind the boxes, where a last-minute practice jump had been erected by a thoughtful owner, he went without demur.

She set him at the jump, and he took it as if he knew he was on trial, although there was only Branch to watch, and as Susan experienced the exquisite freedom of that smooth and lovely flight her last qualms deserted her. She put him at it again, but he did not seem to need her guidance or encouragement. He jumped obligingly and light-heartedly. Branch was admiringly profane about him.

They spent so long playing with him that they almost missed their turn and came up to join the others at the gate just as the first rider muffed the wall and rode off to the exit on the opposite side of the ring, disqualified.

Geraldine was fourth on the list, but she found time to sidle over to Susan. Her eyes were bright and suspicious.

"Whose horse is that?" she demanded brusquely, the briefness of the moment robbing her of even the semblance of courtesy.

Susan sighed. Her heart was warm.

"Phil Birlingstone's," she said. "He asked me if I'd take him round as a special favour. Isn't he sweet? — The...the horse, I mean."

"Naturally," said Geraldine sharply and her expression was dangerous. "The horse seems all right. Phil is a little trusting, isn't he?"

She turned and rode away, but Susan was not even momentarily annoyed. She was very, very happy.

Bitter Aloes entered the ring on her toes. She was proud and black and beautiful. On her back rode Geraldine, firm and capable, and looking in her intense irritation rather magnificent.

The first two brushwood fences were taken without a fault. Bitter Aloes danced up to them, paused, took off like a rocket and landed gracefully on the other side.

The gate, too, in all its frightening whiteness, was negotiated with style and distinction. So was the wall with the unpleasant loose bricks on top.

The crowd at the grandstand murmured its approval. Only once, at the penultimate jump, did the wand fall. The flying hooves passed a fraction too near the pole and the wand, lying loose upon it, fluttered to the ground behind them. Geraldine looked round, saw it, and said something short and spiteful. Bitter Aloes seemed to feel her failure and made a special effort at the final jump. She took off like a bird, cleared the water and the sand, and landed sweetly on the turf, to trot off to the exit with only a single point against her.

Susan was still marvelling at the grace of that performance when she heard her own number called. Branch led her to the gates.

"Good luck, Miss. A clean round and you'll do it," he murmured.

The steward motioned her forward and they came out alone into the great ring with the formidable array of obstacles around it. She touched the roan gently with her heels.

"Now, darling," she whispered.

And then, of course, it happened. Sweet and Low became aware of the crowds and the shining motorcars midway between the entrance and the first jump. He stopped dead, throwing Susan up his neck, and surveyed them, not with fear but with tremendous satisfaction.

After chivalrously waiting for her to wriggle back into the saddle he gave a little squeal and a buck of sheer pleasure and set off for the first jump like an express train.

He took it so high that Susan felt they must never come down and steeled herself to steady him. But he did not need or notice her ministrations.

Having accomplished what he had set out to do, he looked back at the fence with so natural a movement that a spontaneous burst of laughter ran round the ring. Unfortunately the sound was music in his ears.

He began to dance a little, not nervously or angrily but with a deliberate and wicked attempt to show off.

With her cheeks burning with shame and embarrassment, Susan tried to control him, but that soft responsive mouth which had seemed so sympathetic in the meadow was now made of solidified rubber. He was utterly unaware of her. His eyes were on the delighted and partially derisive crowd and his ears were strained toward them.

He took the next hedge sideways. It was a miraculous performance because he did not break it. He actually cleared it, landing broadside on with a neigh that startled every other horse on the ground.

This time the laughter became a little hysterical and Sweet and Low lost his head. He stood in the fairway, neighing, until the judge's megaphone bellowed to Susan to complete her round. She was almost in tears. Her crop made no impression on the roan. He was drunk with the sense of his own cleverness and had no mind for anything else in the world.

She was just wondering if she ought to get down and try to lead him out when he seemed to sense that he was losing his audience. He put down his head, saw the gate, disliked it, and bolted round it, flipping it neatly over with his heels as he passed.

The wall he charged.

Susan was terrified. In the split second before the crash she saw the horse lying in the heap of debris with herself beneath him. But she had reckoned without his peculiar dramatic sense. He came to rest with his forelegs on the top of the wall and, after he had heard the laughter, he beat it down systematically and picked his way over the remaining board or two as daintily as if he were coming down the gangway of his box.

The next jump he cleared as gracefully and stylishly as Bitter Aloes had done, but without displacing the wand.

Susan was deaf and blind with misery. The crowd was a swimming mass of spitefulness and the creature beneath her a fiend in equine shape.

She set him at the water-jump, and he played his last card. He unseated her. He did it quite deliberately in a neat calculating fashion that was positively insulting.

He stopped to pitch her up his neck just before the take-off and then soared into the air, putting in a diabolical wriggle under the saddle which shot her squarely into the water. He landed gracefully, shook himself, and had the effrontery to come back and watch her clambering out.

Susan grasped his bridle amid general laughter, hand-clapping and hysterical badinage.

Sweet and Low walked placidly beside her wet and bedraggled little figure. Just before they reached the exit, he threw up his head and omitted one last paralysing neigh.

They were all waiting for her as she came through the gates, a smiling Geraldine, a Phil who was not smiling, a grey-faced Branch, Tony and Jean, Jean in tears, and little Bill, Susan's small cousin, clutching Taffy.

Susan only saw Phil. She led Sweet and Low up to him. She was shaken, humiliated, and as angry as it is possible for a young woman to be.

"Here's your horse," she said. "I won't tell you what I think of either of you. You're both clowns; filthy, cruel, not at all funny clowns, and I hope you both laugh yourselves to death."

"Susan, I didn't know…" Phil's voice began, but Geraldine's clear, ringing voice drowned the latter part of his sentence.

"Wildly funny," she said.

Susan ignored her. She felt her face was muddy and her clothes were clinging to her. She looked Phil full in the eyes.

"You did know," she said, and, swinging herself on to Taffy's back, rode out of the ground amid ribald inquiries and commiserations from the hangers-on.

They were trotting smartly down the Finchingtree road and had just turned onto the Heath. Susan was permitting the tears to run freely down her muddy cheeks when Sweet and Low overtook them.

He came bounding along happily, his ears forward and his white eye-patch glistening rakishly in the sun.

Susan was so surprised to see his leering head come up beside her that she forgot to wipe her tears away before glancing at his rider.

Phil was very grave and a trifle pale. He was also breathless and wore no hat.

"This beast is mad," he said abruptly as Sweet and Low dropped into step beside Taffy and made a sly but unsuccessful attempt to tweak the green rosette from the pony's headband. "He's just jumped the bonnet of a car."

"Where?" demanded Susan stupidly, startled out of her fury by the sensational news.

"Coming out of the ground. Thank God it was stationary." Phil was breathing heavily. "I've lost my hat and my crop and my nerve. I say, Susan..."

Susan looked away. She felt deeply disillusioned, elderly and cynical.

"I don't want to hear the joke explained," she said briefly. "In fact, I may be quite without humour, but I don't want to speak to you again, ever. Keep that brute away from Taffy! He's got his mane now."

There was a scuffle beside her, and she dug her heels into the pony's sides. He trotted on obligingly but started and kicked out as a strawberry muzzle playfully nipped his plump quarter as he passed. Susan's anger blazed. She swung round, her face flushed and her eyes dangerously bright.

"Keep him away!" she exploded. "Haven't you done enough without persecuting us? Keep him away!"

She caught a glimpse of Phil's lean face as he struggled with that mouth of iron. It was long and somehow faintly pathetic.

"I can't, woman! Can't you see I can't?" he said with sudden and uncharacteristic helplessness. "Oh, Susan, have a heart."

Susan reined Taffy and sat staring up at Sweet and Low's rider. Sweet and Low himself was now blowing ingratiatingly at the pony, who showed signs of being beguiled.

"You knew what was going to happen," she said accusingly. "You knew this beast was a rogue...no, not a rogue, perhaps, but a clown, anyway. You knew it."

Phil nodded gravely. "I guessed. He played the fool with me over at Tony's place. Some school-children climbed on the paddock rails and as soon as he saw them, he began to behave like a lunatic. That was why I wriggled out of riding him. I'm terrified of him! He's possessed."

"Then why thrust him on to me?" Susan was quivering.

"I didn't, darling, I didn't." Phil was evidently unaware of the endearment. "I had no idea. He behaves as if he had been trained in a circus. I thought Tony had found out I was scared stiff of the creature. I dropped him a broad hint last night. I thought he was trying to let me down lightly so that he could get Geraldine to take the beast round. That's why I played up when Jean put over a heart-attack that wouldn't have fooled a convocation of lay-readers."

Susan's eyes snapped.

"Do you think Geraldine could have got him over those jumps this afternoon?"

Phil shrugged his shoulders. He looked wretched.

"No. But it wouldn't have hurt her to try. She likes difficult horses. She's so fearless and all that."

Susan forgot herself.

"I hate fearless women," she declared.

"So do I," echoed Phil fervently. "I loathe them. They terrify me."

Susan was gaping at him, but he went on doggedly.

"I'm going to make a confession to you. I never told this to another soul because I'm naturally pretty ashamed of it, but I must tell you, because if it hadn't been true, I'd never have let you in for that filthy experience this afternoon. I'm a horse funk. That's why I stick to them. I hate being afraid. Every time I take a dirty jump my stomach turns over. That point-to-point I won frightened me out of my wits. When I saw you among those rabbit-holes that day I yelled at you in pure terror and you were naturally livid with me. So, when I suspected what this creature was capable of, I felt I'd rather crawl under the car and die than take him into the ring. I thought either Geraldine would master him and enjoy it, or he'd master her and enjoy it. I didn't care which way it went. But when I got out of my car and saw you up, I nearly passed out. I'm sorry, Susan."

Susan looked at Sweet and Low. He had now achieved Taffy's rosette and was eating it thoughtfully.

"You got up on him to come after me?" she remarked.

Phil stared unhappily. He looked the most dejected object on earth.

"I had to tell you," he said. "I had to explain. It's bad enough to have you snubbing me every time you see me without knowing that you think I'm a louse as well."

Susan was suddenly wildly and unreasonably happy. Her worldliness dropped from her shoulders, leaving her with a slightly irresponsible feeling of childlike satisfaction. With true feminine illogicality she discovered a violent sympathy with the villain of the piece.

"He's not a bad horse," she said rubbing a small muddy hand over the roan's white eye. "Rather sweet."

"And low," said Phil feelingly.

"I like him," Susan persisted obstinately. "Would Tony sell him?"

Phil took her hand and looked at it for a long time.

"He might part up with him as a wedding present," he said with unconvincing casualness. "Shall we put it up to him?"

Susan looked up.

And then, of course, both horses started to gallop, but no one could blame them. It is a time-honoured signal.

ONCE IN A LIFETIME

Beth La Verne settled herself in the railway carriage with the expert care of an experienced theatrical traveller. Judy, her white poodle, lay on the seat, her head on Beth's lap. The rest of the compartment was strewn with bulky hand-luggage sufficient to discourage any but the most determined stranger.

Beth La Verne was thirty-five by her birth certificate and twenty-eight to the agents. In her own way she was successful. Fifteen years of repertory in the big cities of the North had given her experience and a sense of assurance which could have been produced by nothing else.

Her job was at her fingertips. She could study a long part in the intervals of rehearsing another on the afternoon of the first night of a third. She could make over her own stage clothes, transforming the stylish dress of the lively lead in one play into the flashy widow's weeds of another. She was value for any repertory proprietor's money and would be so for another fifteen years.

Beth La Verne was on her way home for a three-day rest before travelling down to Sheepsgate for the southern season that the Old Man was preparing. She had worked for the Old Man for eight years now without a break, which was saying something for he was not particularly fond of her.

Beth La Verne stretched her toes inside her Italian suede shoes like a small black cat. She was very satisfied. She had nothing to grumble about.

Life had its moments. The leading lady of any repertory company is practically certain of a great popularity among the regular patrons of the theatre and Beth La Verne had never quite lost her first thrill at being mobbed in the street, cheered on the first night of each new play and snowed under by showers of silly little presents handed up over the footlights from shy matrons and stage-struck girls.

Backstage it was fashionable to pretend boredom and distaste at these effusions and some in the company were genuinely irritated by the noisy attentions which encroached on their few leisure hours, but in her early days Beth La Verne had revelled in the attention and even after fifteen years still she loved it all. It stimulated and amused her and in some odd way it satisfied her femininity.

She had before her a long journey and she sat looking out at the whirling landscape with placid, introspective eyes. Her thoughts were trivial. The train would stop at the big northwest junction and then it was a straight run. If she could keep the compartment empty at that one stop, she would have it to herself for the rest of the trip and, if she wanted to, poor darling, Judy could stretch her legs. She had a damned good mind to have Judy mated again while they were in Sheepsgate. The last puppies had been a great success, really very lucrative.

Beth La Verne wondered if she would have her hair made fair once more. It was a step she had puzzled over for nearly two weeks. After all, she had been born fair, so it should suit her. But, taking it all in all, dark hair was less trouble and the Old Man did not mind.

The Old Man did not mind anything so long as a girl was keen

on her work and looked passable. She disliked the Old Man
cordially, but there were worse managers. At least his money was
safe.

Beth La Verne glanced down at the book on her knee and
hoped the Sheepsgate Public Library was as efficient as the one
she had just used. She liked a book every two or three days. It
relieved the monotony. She turned the pages over in an idle effort
to find her place. It was another love story, she noticed, and hoped
there was more to it than just that. The public was besotted with
love. Beth La Verne took a professional interest in the thought. It
really was extraordinary how interesting they — those strange,
moon-faced creatures who peopled the rest of the world and
lifted their white countenances to the stage — how incredibly
interesting they found love.

Beth La Verne did not call it sex. Sex was fun. To a leading lady
of "legit" it was love, Love with a capital "L," and was very deep
and emotional and for some reason or other inexplicably sad.

She turned to the end of the book and glanced at the last few
sentences on the last half-page.

"I thought you'd never know. I never meant you to know."

Sir Peter took her in his arms and, because she was only half-complying,
he kissed her hair while her own lips brushed the smooth brown line of
his neck.

"I knew," he said. "I knew, my sweet."

THE END

Beth La Verne smiled considerately. She turned back to page
twenty-four again and read with renewed interest. Sir Peter had
not yet appeared and the heroine, Jennifer, was romping around
with a rather too obvious boy called Dennis.

Beth La Verne hoped there was not going to be anything sordid. Realism was all right, in its place, but nowadays there was altogether too much of it in her opinion.

The word started a train of thought. Realism meant like life, like life really is. Sir Peter wasn't realism. A man didn't take you in his arms and kiss your hair if he suddenly realised he loved you, or if he did it wasn't that you noticed. You noticed something real, like his collar smelling of laundry and you thought of things Jennifer would never dream of thinking about. Thoughts that, now that you'd got him, and he was yours, was it going to be worth it; or was it going to turn into one of those processions beginning with a thousand reawakened vulnerabilities and ending in a chilly conviction that it would have saved a lot of bother if you'd never caught his eye.

That...thought Beth La Verne from the wealth of her experience, that was the realism of love.

She patted the dog's head on her knee and looked out of the window again. Her considerate smile vanished.

It wasn't quite true, of course.

Sometimes, very seldom, once in a lifetime perhaps, people really loved.

Thirty-five-year-old Beth La Verne sat looking at the flying fields and remembered a wet evening far back in the dim days, when Betty Garrod, who had never thought of calling herself Beth La Verne, had sat on the stone porch of the closed Methodist Church in the lane that ran off the High Street. There she had laid her head on the big bony shoulder of the untidy boy who was as wretched as she, before them the wet pavement, brown and liquid as unset toffee, and beyond the grey, mist-hung factory wall with the glistening green leaves of the plane trees against it, as melancholy and as desolate as they.

That had been different.

Jennifer and Sir Peter paled into the absurd beside that, and all the realism that made up Beth La Verne's subsequent experience faded before that one tragically ludicrous picture, so vivid, so excruciating, and so long ago.

They hadn't met again. Parents, another town, a mother who watched the post with a sort of righteous ghoulishness lighting up hard, sophisticated eyes. The gradual realisation that "they" were right, the realisation that one had talent, that there was in front of her a flaming career — Beth La Verne permitted herself a little smile at that — waiting for one if one only worked, all this had dug between them a gulf as wide and intractable as space itself. "They" had been the end of it.

With all the abysmal optimism of youth she had imagined that it would come again, not once but many times, and she had spent the rest of her life making over and over again the exasperating discovery that this was not true.

However, it has existed, that was the main thing. Once it had existed and therefore it could exist again. In other lives, to other people, it could and did exist in all its own untarnishable, imperishable magnificence. It was not a purely transitory dream, a lie told to make life more reasonable. It had solidity and realism, just like the ugly things. Her own real love was long ago and far off, now anything of that kind would be too hopelessly disturbing to be borne, but it had had existence, and the knowledge of that existence was a comforting thing to add to her store of experience, which was so largely made up of far less lovely discoveries.

"Once in a lifetime, once and forever, you and me, me and you, wherever you are, wherever I am, however old, however far, once in a lifetime, once and for ever." The words made a little refrain, like rain on wet pavements.

Beth La Verne laughed at herself and noted that tears on her new mascara made her eyes sticky. She turned again to the library book and read happily about Jennifer and Sir Peter until the train stopped at the junction.

When the heavy, hurrying man threw open the door and thrust two great suitcases into the compartment, knocking her feet, she scowled at him and Judy barked, but the man seemed not to notice, he was too concerned with his comfort and his luggage to be. He moved Beth La Verne's dressing case from the corner diagonally opposite to her and settled himself. The cases he kept where they were, in the well of the floor.

Beth La Verne, who knew when she was beaten, contented herself by closing the door with a slam and pulling up the window with a rattle and a look.

"Sorry," he said and pulled out a newspaper.

The apology seemed to mollify Beth La Verne. She nodded and for a moment her startled dark eyes rested on his face. He began to read, and she took up her book again.

She watched him furtively under lashes as she flicked over the pages with convincing regularity.

Seventeen years alter faces and figures, but not the colour of the eyes or the eccentric tricks, the way people have of moving, sighing, or rubbing the short hairs at the back of their necks with a nervous bony hand.

In the first half-hour Beth La Verne came as near as ever she had come to dithering. This was the sort of meeting she had rehearsed long ago when she was first on the stage and first burning with those fires of drama which the years had doused. Then, she had always imagined it beginning just like this. He wouldn't recognise her at first — after all, her hair was a different colour — and then she'd speak, saying something commonplace but unexpected, like, "My dear, how nice to see you," or "I've altered, haven't I?" And then, then it would all happen.

These had been the rehearsals, of fifteen, fourteen, even as late as ten years ago, but now, sitting in a railway carriage at the age of thirty-five with a dog beside her, a sentimental book on her knee and a job waiting for her, she hesitated and was dumb.

"A heavy weight of hours has chained and bowed..." Beth La Verne could not remember the rest of the poem.

He sat peacefully on the other side of the carriage, concentrating on his newspaper and absent-mindedly caressing the back of his neck with his hand.

He looked kindly and sophisticated. He, too, had gathered experience, no doubt. There was nothing unattractive about him, much that she noticed was improvement. But still she kept her head bent over her book.

Once he spoke to her.

"Mind if I lower this window?"

She nodded again, fearing that her voice would give her away, but she had raised her head and he met her eyes squarely and without expression.

It was her overwhelming relief at that lack of expression which gave her the key to her own state of mind.

If, when she spoke, he recognised her and if, even then, it did not "all happen"? If there followed a few awkward reminiscences, an exchange of cards, and a relieved parting at the terminus? If *that* — that parting in the rain, that sweet two years, that one vital, comforting, significant experience — if that, too, were not real, what then?

Beth La Verne stiffened. It was a risk which she shrank from taking. There was too much to lose.

She turned up her coat collar, huddled herself in the corner, and resolutely read her library book until, at the terminus, Sir Peter took Jennifer into his arms and kissed her hair.

She did not look up until the man had left the carriage.

That evening, at home, the man from the train was suddenly confronted with one of those uncanny intuitions which, with a genius for the opportune, seem to be a prime characteristic of women as habitually trying as his wife. "Do you remember," she said, apropos of nothing, "that girl you used to tell me about before we were married?" and raising her voice above the din of radio music, "You know, the one you said you really loved, your once in a lifetime girl? If you met her now, over fifteen years later, what would you do? Would you still love her?"

The man looked up from the other side of the fireplace, his eyes carefully without expression. There was in his face nothing that revealed the scars of his long ordeal on the train, no sign whatsoever of the emotional suffering that stayed with him from those long hours, but he could not reply immediately.

She looked at him as if she demanded some response. He laughed and rubbed the back of his neck. "I don't know," he said cautiously, "I mean, I'd have to see her properly, talk with her. She's probably changed. Whatever put that into your head?"

His wife smiled. "I don't know," she said. "Must have been the dance music, I suppose. It's extraordinary, isn't it, how interested everyone is in love. No one seems to write or sing about anything else."

THE KERNEL OF TRUTH

Alfred inherited the recipe for Prior's Punch (whose other name in the lost archives was "Liquor of Happiness") and, almost on the same day, *Le Jardin des Enfants Doux* in Siddon's Street, Soho, and, since his was an essentially practical disposition, both were by way of being a responsibility to him.

Des Enfants was out of favour with the Bohemians, who at that far-off time could make or break any eating establishment, the chef was erratic to the point of being a visionary, and the interior was badly in need of re-gilding. Alfred's father had never been remarkable as a restaurateur save in the singular particular that he was an Englishman, and one day he gave up his good-natured muddling and stepped, so to speak, out of one garden into another where, no doubt, the indefatigable Frenchwoman who had been Alfred's mother was awaiting him on the lawns of Paradise.

A little later in the same week, far down in the country, there died also the fabulous great-aunt of whom Alfred had heard so much. In her time she had cooked at great houses where royalty visited. The remnant of her days she had spent in a tied cottage on a fast-dwindling estate. Alfred was her sole remaining relative and, had he been of a less prosaic mind, he might have hoped for his share of the munificence of princes, but, when it arrived in a registered envelope forwarded by the vicar of the parish, his inheritance from his great-aunt consisted of but two treasures. One was a button cut from Bonaparte's coat by an ancestor of the old lady's who had been in service with the governor of St Helena, and the other was a sealed package, labelled simply "It."

Alfred had no doubt that this was the recipe for the punch. He opened it and spread the tattered piece of sermon-paper (or its vellum equivalent) on the cash desk of *Des Enfants*. He had heard so much of the famous draught and its extraordinary properties that, for all his lack of romantic feeling, he could not escape a thrill of anticipation as he saw at last the mystery set forth in a bold and clerkly hand.

Unfortunately, the first item set his feet back firmly on the ground.

"One. Take of finest French brandy thirty years in cask two full quarts and toss it in a silver bowl made hot."

Alfred sighed. As he had feared, the Liquor of Happiness had no great commercial possibilities.

He folded the parchment sadly and placed it with the button, which looked like a medal, and with them the accompanying note which said that anyone who wore the button would "achieve dominance," in the secret drawer of the desk in which he kept the details of his overdraft.

However, after a spring in which *Des Enfants Doux* might well have been *Des Guttersnipes Revolting* for all the notice anyone took of his restaurant, the maternal relatives of Alfred, of whom there were several dozen in the immediate vicinity, made what was for Alfred a fateful decision, and Augustine appeared.

In this important matter Alfred's practical disposition was a great comfort, for at first sight Augustine at twenty-eight was not a vision to quicken the blood. She was thin and sallow with a string nose, a decided chin and little black eyes like sequins. But she brought a *dot* which was timely rather than sizeable and her parents, who kept The Chicken on the Hearth in Caroline Street, were sorry to part with her...save, of course, for her tongue.

The miracle occurred at the wedding. After the ceremony. There were at the breakfast relatives — from both sides — assembled and Augustine, wearing the button of Bonaparte which had been made into a brooch, was sitting in the centre of a smugly speculative throng when, for the first time, Alfred made the Liquor of Happiness.

He made only a half-quantity because, great though the occasion was, there is a difference between generosity and sheer prodigal extravagance, but there was no tampering with the ingredients. All was as laid down. Even the bowl was of solid silver. Mr Reubenstein from the corner, who lent the vessel, came with it, of course, but he had a charming character and a fund of the most delicate and suitable anecdotes and could almost have merited an invitation anyhow.

For Alfred the first intimation of the experience to come — the first few notes on the harp, as it were — began when he first poured the pint of Demerara rum into the quart of tossed brandy and a thin blue air, too rare to be called a fume, arose from a mixture, brown and soft as a passionate eye, in the soft, white metal of the bowl. Immediately a strange new sense of well-being stole over him and, for the first time, he saw the broad flat face of his mother-in-law without any unease whatsoever. He added the ten lemons one by one, rejoicing in their exquisite ripeness and the way the juice hung like mist swirls in the mixture. When first he had read the recipe the demand for powdered white sugar had seemed to him to be too lavish, but he used the full half-pound and, as he breathed the now powerful fragrance, he began to smile and the worries of the past and the apprehensions for the future began to fade.

With the mace and the cinnamon — one penny-weight of each — he began to think of *Des Enfants* as a magnificent possession and, by the time he had added a trace of allspice, the pathway of his life had taken on a certain splendour such as previously he had not observed.

At this point the recipe ended, save for the direction concerning boiling water ("one gallon drawn from a fair spring"), but there was below a single line of writing so faint as to be indecipherable. Alfred gave up trying to read it and added the water which had just come to the boil in a coffee-urn. At once the full melody, as one might say, of the beverage poured out beneath his nose in glorious crescendo.

At that moment he caught sight of his bride and at once he noticed about her something delightful which he had never seen before. Her long spice-brown hair, drawn back with a comb set on the back of her head, had an undulation in its strands that touched his heart and reminded him of something pleasant and familiar. He stood looking at it open-mouthed, and absentmindedly his fingers strayed toward the spice-tray where a packet of nutmegs nestled. Still absorbed by his wife's hair, so like the brown fruit in his hand, he grated a whole small nut into the brew *after* — and this, as it happened, was important — the water had been added.

The rest of the evening was pure magic.

The gathering, made up of experts, was not easy to impress or to soften, but the things that happened that night made talk among them for a decade. Men saw new beauty in the wives of twenty years; children confided in their parents; Mr Reubenstein was actually prevented by the mother of Augustine from presenting the happy couple with the valuable bowl; and an obscure and hitherto neglected uncle sang a song of a far country which no one had ever heard before or could remember afterward, but which was so beautiful that everyone who spoke of it sighed gently and made somebody else a small gift.

That was the first time Alfred made the Liquor of Happiness, and for a very long time he thought it also the last.

Of course, he brewed the punch from the recipe a number of times.

In one sense he prospered. Augustine, with the sign of the dominator, blue and gold, upon her bosom, was the sort of woman who did not countenance failure and, as their joint efforts were poured ruthlessly and untiringly into it, *Des Enfants* waxed in popularity. Alfred made the punch a score of times throughout those years. It shed a scented benison at the christenings of each of his children. The heads of Alfred junior, of Ernestine, of Cecile, of Paul, of Tony, of Bettine and Josef, were all wetted at the conventional times with no less a draught, but never once did it achieve quite the same unearthly potency as had been observed upon that first occasion. It was always remarkable, always admired, but the highest note, the sweet, shrill echo of peace of the heart was never reached again, not until very much later.

It was after the war. Alfred and Augustine were no longer young. The darkness, the noise and the tragedy and hard work had left their mark upon them. One summer's night the *Des Enfants* itself had sunk in black ashes and, but for Augustine's thrift, prudence, and indomitable courage, it might never have arisen again. Then, one Sunday in the early 1950s, in the new and recently enlarged *Des Enfants,* white walled and decked with blushing napery, Alfred made the punch again.

It was his silver wedding and there were a great many guests. He stood behind the table with the pink cloth on it and with a delicate hand poured four bottles *of fine* into his own silver bowl. Ernestine, Cecile and Bettine waited upon him and, far across the graceful room, Augustine sat stiffly among her guests, the button of Bonaparte her only jewel.

In many respects it was a splendid affair and most eyes in the assembly were envious, but Alfred, catching sight of himself in a mirror, felt vaguely resentful. He saw a fat man with a short neck and insufficient hair. It was only to be expected, he told himself sensibly as he stirred in the sugar and took up the small wooden box of powdered allspice. Life had been hard and Augustine's tongue one of its many scourges. Youth had come and looked at him, had sighed and gone away.

It was sad, he reflected, sad but inevitable. He glanced across at Augustine and frowned. She was a remarkable woman, indefatigable and, but for that one failing, a good enough sort, her failing that she had never been a beauty. Now, with her sallow skin, dusted with a powder too pale, her little eyes and her wrinkles, she looked like nothing so much as a nutmeg.

He was so struck by the similarity that, without realising what he was doing, he took one from the box and grated almost the whole of it into the punch. The bitter flakes lay on the steaming surface of the pool like dust on mahogany. Startled, he stood back and nodded to his elder daughter to begin to serve.

The miracles of middle age happen slowly. The proprietor of *Des Enfants Doux* had reached the bottom of his first rummer before it occurred to him that something very remarkable had taken place. He observed the phenomenon when, on looking in the glass, he saw not a fat man, but a stalwart blessed with becoming dignity, interestingly grey.

As he lifted his head, he heard for the first time in twenty-five years a deep warm note in the chatter about him and his heart leapt. Quite suddenly Bettine, who was in love as well — with Jules, the new *sommelier* — achieved beauty. It blossomed before her father's astounded eyes like a Japanese paper flower unfolding in a glass of water. Even Ernestine, who took after her mother's family, had a radiance that Alfred had never seen before.

The entire company underwent a strange, unforgettable experience in which only the very best in the nature of each enjoyed a sweet liberation. Later on in the evening someone sang a song everybody remembered hearing long ago, but none knew when or where.

It had happened again. The Liquor of Happiness had been achieved a second time.

Even the next day when, in the break after their late luncheon in a corner of the deserted restaurant, Alfred and Augustine discussed it, the affair remained with them as slightly uncanny. Alfred was inclined to put it down to the quality of the brandy, but when they sent for a bottle of the same brand it was no better and no worse than the *fine* that they had used so often.

"Think!" commanded Augustine, her sharp eyes earnest. "Without doubt it is a matter of mixing! Think! First at our wedding and then again last night."

Alfred allowed his practical mind to dwell on the two occasions.

"Wait," he said suddenly. "That's it. It's something to do with you. Each time at the very end of the business, after the water has gone in, I caught sight of you and…" He paused abruptly.

His wife stared at him. "Perhaps you've been drinking too much?" she suggested coldly.

"No." Alfred was on the right track, but he perceived a difficulty. "No, my dear. It's a fact. That's the only difference. On each of these special occasions, just as the stuff was ready, I looked over at you and — er — something happened."

Augustine flushed, and her sequin eyes grew ever brighter. "Idiot!" she said, but she was very pleased and when she got up to go over to the account books, she let a brown hand rest caressingly for a moment on his collar. "The mother of Jules is coming to speak to you tonight about Bettine," she murmured. "He's a good worker. Let us hope they are as happy as we have been. 'The look of love' eh? You old *blagueur!* That was the secret, was it?"

She went off laughing, and, left to himself, to settle his digestion Alfred took a small glass of the *fine*.

He reflected that Augustine was a good woman and the best wife in the world — but for her failing. Her last words were still in his ears and under his breath he answered them. He was a kindly man if a practical one. "It wasn't, you know," he said to himself. "It was the nutmeg."

HAPPY CHRISTMAS

Young Mr and Mrs Robinson collected Victoriana and considered collecting it their Thing. He was tall, dark, very good-looking and without fault save a quick temper, she was a roly-poly duck of a girl with spun gold hair and bright eyes, and she was, just a little, what used to be called a muggins. Let us face that fact, accept it, and ignore it. He was twenty-four, she twenty-one and their son Sebastian fifteen months and four days old.

The Robinsons took their hobbies seriously. They did not live but rather resided in the basement flat of one of those high, terrace houses which stand like vast, keg moulded butter-lamps along the endless stone shelves of London's wide western streets north of the park. It was certainly no mansion flat, but the principal room was sufficiently large to house the dining table and the splendid set of six chairs which had launched the couple into the mysteries of collecting, and also the love seat, not much use for loving but superb for quarrelling.

Outside the flat there was a tiny triangle of garden for Sebastian and the Good Dog Tray, large enough to house also Sebastian's pram, if only after Michael's rages had persuaded the local urchins that it was not a litter bin or a receptacle for amazingly expensive toys intended for Sebastian's use.

The GD Tray was a pleasing dog, brownish, fat, with a round head, beautiful eyes and a leg at each corner.

On the evening before Christmas Eve there was crisis in their cosy room with the sprigged paper which Mr Robinson had hung with his own hands.

As so often in this modern world, it was the telephone which served as herald to crisis. The Robinsons' telephone, for all that it was disguised by a knitted tea-cosy so that it would not clash with the fine group of waxed flowers and fruits under a glass dome which stood beside it, remained a telephone still and still possessed of all that instrument's faults and so it was that when it rang, late in that evening of December 23rd, not only did it set Sebastian in his early, ironwork cot to howling, but also, in its habitually abrupt and abominable off-hand way, it announced that Moppet and Mo would not, after all, spend Christmas with their second-degree friends the Robinsons. At the last minute they had been summoned to a supersession at Castle Croesus; miraculously their car had recovered its health; they were off first thing in the morning; Mo was taking his guitar.

For themselves, Moppet and Mo were no great loss, but they were the only people known to the Robinsons who had not planned to leave London over Christmas. Mr Robinson was the child of a broken home; his parents had given him an expensive education and a little money, then fled from each other and from him to establish new families in distant countries. Mrs Robinson's widowed mother was off in Australia with Mrs Robinson's sister and it was from that land of fruits that there had arrived, already at the end of November, the stupendous hamper which the Robinsons planned to use as substance of the feast which now Moppet and Mo had spurned.

Mr Robinson slammed down the phone and, forgetting to replace its cover, spoke his thoughts about Moppet and Mo.

Sebastian continued to howl. Mrs Robinson howled too and blamed all on her husband. Only the delights of reconciliation put them at last to sleep.

But on Christmas Eve morning the tragedy was inescapable. Not just one major tragedy but a whole series of tragedies. Mr Robinson had bought for himself a plum-coloured smoking jacket with a black-quilted collar and frogging. It would set off his slim figure, his black curls and moustache, but he could not cut a dash without an audience. Mrs Robinson had hidden, in a box under their bed, the find of all finds, a genuine Victorian smoking cap, plum-coloured like Mr Robinson's jacket and like that jacket frogged, and she knew, but did not tell that she knew, that there was another package under the bed. She had not looked at it, that would be cheating, but it felt like the glass lily bases which had disappeared so recently from Levein's window. And Mrs Robinson had a new dress in stiff, check silk, her "new best tabby" which, no less than Mr Robinson's smoking jacket, deserved and needed an admiring audience.

Now everything was spoiled. To comfort him Mrs Robinson reminded her husband that, "because you are so good at it," he was going to cook the goose. Mr Robinson flared; the goose had already been cooked, and by Mo, damn him! They might just as well stay in bed and forget all about Christmas.

Mrs Robinson burst into tears again. She had tried not to, but she was that sort of girl and that, after all, was why he loved her. She wailed that, this first Christmas after the end of rationing, she had set her heart on a truly Victorian Christmas.

Mr Robinson smacked his hand on the mantle and broke one of their prized Staffordshire greyhounds. "Damn Queen Victoria," he said, frightening even himself by *lèse-majesté* so out-of-place in that household and, in that moment, divorce, dissolution, death and the end of the world were all imminent.

Suddenly Mrs Robinson had an idea. Like all of those "Mugginses" she was on occasion visited by a flash of pure genius.

"Everybody in the house is going away for Christmas. Everybody, except the old woman on the top floor. She's a genuine Victorian. We can't have our party, but we could ask her in — sort of, have a rehearsal — find out from her what a Victorian Christmas really was like, so that we get it dead right another time."

Mr Robinson was dubious. The old woman they saw sometimes crawling up the stone stairs to the porch above their kitchen was not notable for friendliness or charm. Had she not given to Mrs Robinson a pretty dusty answer when Mrs Robinson, seeing her so tired, had offered to carry her shopping-bags? No, they might as well throw Sebastian and the GD Tray into the Serpentine, go off to the Two Corporals, and get gloriously drunk.

He did not go to the Serpentine. He did not go to the pub. Instead he went to the Sunday market in Praed Street. Common decency demanded that he collect the large bunch of holly and the discreet sprigs of mistletoe which they had ordered.

When he returned there was the Victorian already installed and an alarming piece of stiff-backed bric-à-brac she seemed.

Miss Martindale was a small woman with crisp grey hair. Her black skirt and twin-set were not out of the ordinary but the gleam in her grey eyes and the firmness of her small mouth announced that this was a woman to be reckoned with.

Mr Robinson was glad to see that his wife seemed content; for himself, he knew that Authority had arrived and that, whether he liked it or not, his Christmas was about to be organised for him, but Mr Robinson did not lack courage. He made one last stand for freedom.

"My wife," he said, "loves everything Victorian, but I don't think we want stuffiness and I don't think we want sentimentality."

To his relief Authority agreed and from then on, she showed toward him more than a hint of flattering deference.

Miss Martindale admired the room and especially the maple-framed colour-prints. Their Landseer was so good, she said, their

Rivière so cosily indifferent. And she was no less definite about the Christmas arrangements. The strengths of the Victorians were three, she remarked, and she spoke in capitals as one who knew: Common Sense, Knowing One's Own Mind, and Thrift. Nothing, but nothing whatsoever, which was valuable, entertaining or nutritious must ever be wasted.

The Robinsons were surprised: they had not associated such a depressing set of virtues with the warmth and reckless abandon of the Christmas saturnalia, but they were captivated by her certainty. The modern world cannot resist the appeal of the expert and here it was to the nth degree in the voice of Miss Martindale. They settled to obedience on all things.

They must hurry. Everything for a proper Victorian Christmas must be ready by 10 pm for, of course, they must all go to the Midnight Service at St Nicholas in Charlotte Place. At St Nicholas, said Miss Martindale, thank goodness, they knew what they were doing. That was a true church for the Victorians, built in the last years of the Regency but recently redecorated in gold and exquisite blue. There would be no crib but there would be the Picture (again the capital!), a genuine Roger der Weyden. They must all sit as close to it as they could to admire Our Lady and the Babe under the Netherlands thatched roof. And all the little angels, leaving behind their vapour trails in the cold, clear air, like tiny airplanes. Next, they must turn their eyes to the two great He-angels on either side of the huge, mahogany alcove and must listen to the blazingly triumphant music pouring, so it seemed, from their Bach trumpets.

The Robinsons were swept along by her certainty and enthusiasm but suddenly Mrs Robinson came to earth. There was in her voice a note of disappointment. "We can't go to church; there's Sebastian, you see."

For a moment even Miss Martindale was dashed but, like a true Victorian, she rose to the occasion. How silly of her to forget that their Emma was a washing-up machine, not so hard, perhaps, on the crockery as all those Emmas of the past but lacking some of their skill and uses. No matter, the Robinsons must go to church; she, Miss Martindale, would protect her bronchitis against the night air. She would sit here by the fire listening to the dog. "Christmas Eve, so, like all the animals, he'll talk his head off at midnight!"

Almost seduced by this surprising offer, still the Robinsons protested but Miss Martindale was gently insistent. They must go. It was essential, a part of the spell to raise the Good Spirits and without those Good Spirits it was quite impossible to celebrate anything, however marvellous.

So Mr and Mrs Robinson went to St Nicholas, saw the Picture, heard the trumpets and came back laughing, bright-eyed and as exalted as Miss Martindale had confidently expected, through a night of cut-diamond stars.

They crept down the area-steps so as not to wake Sebastian and found Miss Martindale in a bright red dressing gown, her hair in curlers, nodding by the gas fire with the GD Tray sitting on her lap, and behind them the greyhounds and the marble clock. It was a scene from the *Illustrated London News* circa 1860.

Miss Martindale made to go home, shy, as Mr Robinson surmised, at being seen in curlers, but she gave in to his blandishment and stayed to show them how to make negus — sherry, boiling water, lemon, sugar, nutmeg and "yes, half a glass of Three Star brandy from your medicine cabinet."

It was a pleasant drink, warming and slightly mysterious. The Robinsons told Miss Martindale about church then asked how she had fared. Had Sebastian cried? Had the GD Tray spoken; if so, what had he said and was it polite?

No, the child hasn't stirred. Yes, the dog had spoken. Miss Martindale stroked his round head affectionately. What did they expect? All the usual things, of course, about him being the Leader of the Pack. Did they not know: on Christmas Eve at midnight when they were allowed to speak, cows told sentimental stories, donkeys droned on and on about their patience, horses were too wise or too proud to speak at all, but dogs...! Dogs came out with those sane, eternal preoccupations which filled their minds through all the year. "If you doubt it, just watch your dog any evening as he dreams by the fire."

They looked in on Sebastian in his cot, set beside him the carefully wrapped presents he was still too young to appreciate, and then Miss Martindale left. But not before she had issued orders for the day: a long lie-in, a light breakfast, time for cooking and preparation, a glass of wine before the Feast. "And, of course," said Miss Martindale, her diction splendidly Victorian, "and, of course, we must hear the dear Queen."

There was no snow that Christmas morning, but the sharp frost made a fine substitute. Everything went according to plan. It was one of Sebastian's good days and he played contentedly with the Victorian Folly his mother had found for him, a musical-box-on-a-stick, until he tired himself out and could be returned to his cot.

The sweet, cool voice of Majesty lent depth, tone and solidity to the proceedings. The first glasses of Portuguese Rosé were raised to "The Queen, God bless her" and they were just about to sit to lunch when the day's first shadow crossed Mrs Robinson's face.

The table looked lovely. The Victorian brass-column lamp with its glass-lace shade made a centre-piece to crow about. But there were six dining-chairs and, even if one counted Sebastian, only four people!

Again Miss Martindale rose to meet crisis. There were always present at a Victorian Christmas dinner a few stuffy relatives. It was a matter of course, part of the ritual. "Why don't we stuff two?"

So they did, and in the process almost had hysterics. While Mr Robinson dished up the goose, made the rum sauce and with a pair of butter-patters banged the plum pudding into the proper Victorian football shape, Uncle and Aunt Dowsett were born.

Uncle Dowsett wore an old pair of Mr Robinson's flannel-trousers and a grey pullover, Aunt Dowsett Mrs Robinson's short dressing gown. Their substance — pillows and sofa cushions — was inclined to be exuberant, their heads — balloons stolen from the decorations — were apt to come adrift with the slightest draft, but they were credible. They delighted Sebastian when he was returned to the party and soon, they took on personalities very much their own.

Miss Martindale, who herself looked something of a sketch in her lace cap and frizzy curls, was just a little catty about them, if in a severely Victorian manner. "Sephronia never lets him speak," she confided to Mr Robinson in a stage whisper. "But you'll see, before the evening is over, he'll become a little inebriated, then he'll break out and embarrass us all with one of those vulgar songs of his."

"Dear lady," protested Mr Robinson, "at Christmas we must be charitable," and he filled Uncle Dowsett's glass.

It was not easy to think of anything decently vulgar for Uncle Dowsett but after the port Mr Robinson had an idea. He rummaged among their old records. There it was, and there was Uncle Dowsett, the record player under his chair, singing "Hallelujah, I'm a Bum" in broad American. Not Victorian, true, but assuredly suited to Uncle Dowsett and sufficiently vulgar to make Mrs Robinson giggle.

Miss Martindale tried to look down her nose, then at last she laughed, and tears came into her eyes.

It had been a glorious meal. The table was littered with wrappings, presents and dessert. Suddenly there was a loud knocking at the door.

What with the love seat and six of them round the dining table the back legs of Miss Martindale's chair were almost on the doormat and she alone could get to the door.

The Robinsons and the Dowsetts heard her clear voice talking to someone outside. "Whatever next? On Christmas Day! Well, really I don't know, but you had better come in and speak to the Master." Then she slipped back in and there filed in after her three horrid, dirty little boys.

They edged round the table and stood in a row, clearly impressed by Mr Robinson's splendid presence, their eyes widening as they noticed his smoking jacket and smoking cap, then rolling as they noticed all the wonders of that room.

Mr Robinson, kindly and paternal, asked them their business and the middle-sized boy, obviously the brains of the gang, announced in a shrill voice, his Cockney only partly schooled by much listening to the BBC, that they were out selling seats for their Christmas play. He proved it by producing a handful of grubby tickets, typed in sticky purple.

He was close to making an immediate sale, but Mr Robinson was Something in the City and therefore in the habit of looking at what it was he was asked to buy. Even whilst he was feeling in his pocket for money, he read a ticket. His handsome face looked pale, his eyes narrowed, and the widow's peak of his forehead came down to meet the bridge of his nose. "You beastly little crooks," he flared. "The performance was the night before last. You picked these tickets off the floor. Look, there's a foot-mark on this one."

It was frightening and frightful, the spell of Christmas shattered, it seemed beyond repair, and a chill wind blew through the room. The Dowsetts looked vacuous, Mrs Robinson turned white, Sebastian wrinkled his nose and opened his mouth enormously to yell and the GD Tray set up a howl.

Miss Martindale swelled into Awful Authority. "Bad Spirits!" she exclaimed in a terrifying voice. "Goodness gracious! What have we let into the house?" She turned on the spokesman. "Tell me, you with the pudding still round your mouth. What parts did you three take in your Christmas play? The wicked angels, no doubt."

Two of the visitors crumpled there and then but Mastermind faced her, angel-eyed and steeped in sin. "No, Miss. We was the Three Kings. I was Melky-Haw. I give the gold."

"So!" Authority was suitably impressed. "That," she said to the Robinsons, "is a case of a different order. Misrepresentations by Small Fiends only, I think, but nonetheless demanding drastic modes of exorcism."

It took even Miss Martindale some time to persuade Mr Robinson to accept the logic of the subsequent business negotiations. It worked, she argued, on the same principle as correcting a skid by turning with it. He who was humiliated by robbery could erase the shame only if he managed to reduce the robber to ridiculous nothing and for *that* the recipe was to force upon the brute, the greedy beast, an unsolicited gift.

All the time fascinated by her reasoning at last Mr Robinson agreed, and the deal was settled: seven-pence for each of the brats. And between them one orange, a stick of cinnamon and one black olive.

The Spirit of Christmas returned to the room. The false Caspar and Balthazar trooped off, greatly relieved and still watery, but Melky-Haw was made of sterner stuff. He shepherded the other two Small Fiends into the area then back to Authority, gave her an angel's smile, and laid before her one of his seven pennies.

"A gift for the By-bee," he said.

Quick as lightning Miss Martindale snatched his grubby hand and emptied it of all his money. "You may keep the orange. Now be off with you or I shall kiss you under the mistletoe."

Before this dread threat the demon fled, banging the door behind him so hard that the draft blew off Sephronia's head.

Aunt Dowsett re-headed, Sebastian back in his cot and fast asleep, and the washing-up gurgling in Emma's mechanical belly, somewhat shamefacedly the Robinsons lifted the Royal Stuart travelling-rug from their brand-new television-set. They were much relieved when Miss Martindale gave it as her firm opinion that television was nothing more than a latter-day Magic Lantern if happily without the associated smell of scorching black Japan.

Miss Martindale loved-and-left. She climbed the stairs to her white walled, uncluttered room, took off her lace, brushed out her curls, and put on her wedding ring. She could never wear it on weekdays; those damned old fogies who ran the gallery where she had worked for years still preferred unmarried employees. Then she mixed herself a very dry Martini, lit a cigarette, and stretched out luxuriously on her severe divan.

It had been a very happy Christmas, she decided. Just one bad moment, and even that somehow bitter-sweet. When Uncle Dowsett had suddenly burst into song she had almost *seen* her dear Old Bill. Poor Bill, mangled in one war, killed when fire-watching in the next and in the years between so often troubled by unemployment; she remembered him singing that Bum song, his young-old face as scarlet as a pillar box, to five or six of them. She had been lolling under the willows. The hot summer of 1933, or was it 1936? She had thought of it from time to time but never as vividly as tonight. Tonight her spine had tingled as she felt his arm about her shoulders; tonight she had felt his breath in her ear.

She sighed, then laughed. Those Robinsons were rather darlings and she was particularly glad to have wiped out that most unfortunate snub she had given to Mrs Robinson earlier in the year. Face it, it was only natural for a girl to assume that a tired woman was too decrepit to carry a shopping basket. When you are twenty anyone who can give you thirty years appears to be as old as God. Fifty-five or one hundred and five. What is there in it?

She listened contentedly to Bach on the radio and again went over the day's celebrations.

It had been a blow missing St Nicholas, but it had been worth it. She thought again of Old Bill. No one had understood parties better than Old Bill but even he, who believed implicitly and at times exasperatingly in the essential gaiety of life, had never been forced to attempt the impossible. One just could not celebrate gloriously if alone. For the water to turn to wine there must be others present. It was a recipe for Christmas as precise and as practical as Mrs Beeton's instructions for preparing negus.

Mercifully, it was laid down for all time, and after. The Original Briefing: "Gang up, no less than two or three!"

THE WISDOM OF ESDRAS

Joseph Berrie put down his newspaper, helped himself to a piece of toast and smiled across at his sister Celia, who sat at the head of the breakfast table.

"Vance is late this morning," he observed, "never in all my life knew such a beggar for his bed hello! Good morning, Vance, come and have some breakfast."

"Morning," returned Bobby Vance as he seated himself.

Celia smiled at him over the tea things. "Help yourself to an egg," she said, "you'll find one on the side. Did you have a good night?"

"Definitely! Slept like a top, but who's the lady in the lilac dress and the infernally noisy shoes?"

Berrie looked up from his eggs. "Who's been spinning you yarns?" he said slowly.

Vance looked at him wonderingly. "No one," he said at last, "but I don't understand you, who is she?"

Celia laughed. "Well, I suppose you'd call her a ghost," she said, "but I can assure you, she's quite harmless. I've seen her heaps of times and Joe hears her often, but the worst of it is he can't see anything and, in fact, he's just a wee bit sceptical. Aren't you, Joe dear?"

Berrie grunted. "I admit there is something roaming about," he said, "but if it is, as you claim, a ghost, why on earth can't you leave the poor thing alone? She does no harm to anyone."

Celia laughed. "Poor old Joe!" she exclaimed. "Just because he can't see her, he hates to talk about her, it's downright pique on his part. Never mind Joe, old boy, you hear her dainty little shoes, don't you?"

Berrie went on with his egg in silence.

Celia turned to Vance. "You know it's funny," she said, "there have been two or three people who have stayed down here who have been unable to see her, even when they have been in the same room as those who have. You're obviously one of the lucky ones."

Vance looked from one to the other in amazement. "Good lord!" he said at last. "Are you really serious? Or are you kidding me? Do you honestly mean to tell me that the little girl in mauve I met last night, and in my pyjamas, is a real genuine ghost?" And then, as he saw on both their faces a similar expression, he added, "I say, how delightful! This is the first time I've ever come up against a real spook. Quite an adventure."

Berrie eyed him inquiringly, almost coldly. "What did she look like?"

"Oh, just a girl in a mauve, fluffy sort of frock, you know, all frilly things down the skirt; and a weird shawl over her shoulders."

Celia looked across at her brother and nodded meaningfully.

"You see," Vance continued, warming to his subject as he recalled slowly, one after another, the incidents of his last night's adventure. "You see, I heard someone crying and then the sound of high-heeled shoes clicking on the stairs. So I got out of bed and went to the door. And then I saw her." He said it with what, almost unconsciously, Berrie thought to be unpardonable pride. "I saw her; just at the bottom of the stairs, by that door that leads into the yard. She had her back to me and her face between her hands. I thought it was you at first," he grinned as he turned to Celia, "and I didn't know what to say; but when she went on crying, I asked her if I could help. She turned, and I saw it wasn't you. Well, then — er — I was a bit shaken, so I started down the stairs after her. She opened the door, I followed, and she disappeared."

"Were you frightened?" asked Berrie as he finished his toast.

Vance flushed. "My dear fellow," he said simply, "I've just told you, I had no idea she was a ghost. Why should I be frightened?"

There was an awkward pause during which Berrie helped himself to another piece of toast.

Vance broke the silence and in his usually boyish tone remarked, "I say, isn't there any old story about the lady? This place seems fairly new, but yet you'd think..."

"Oh yes! There is a story," Celia interposed. "Ages ago, Merley used to be a real old smuggling centre. That old barn affair over there in the garden used to be the Old Bell Inn, a sort of general headquarters for all the villains of the neighbourhood. They say that she was a girl who found out about the smuggling trade and that eventually she decided to show them up, although her father, or her lover, or someone was in it too. She disappeared mysteri- ously, killed most probably by these people, and she's haunted the place ever since. It isn't the old inn itself, however, she never goes past our doorway; it's the ground outside, so when they built this cottage it was this place she haunted."

"I say, what a brilliantly exciting sort of lady," said Vance. "I hope I see her again."

Berrie pushed away his plate and got up. "Well, I'm going down to Hughes, to see about that boat. Celia will tell you dozens of creepy stories, if you let her; she's simply shot full of them, but if I were you, I'd play tennis instead. It's healthier." He stepped through the French windows and strolled across the garden.

"Ghosts are funny things," Vance remarked. "I used to think they were all bosh till I read those books by old Oliver Lodge. Even then I wasn't quite sure. But now, of course, there's no doubt about it — I've seen one."

"Oh, I've believed in ghosts all my life," said Celia. "You see, we've had this cottage for the summer ever since we were kids. She's always been here, of course. Mother could see her, but Dad was like Joe, he could only hear her. I know Mother used to tell how sometimes of an evening she and Dad used to sit in the dining room with me, when I was a baby, and they would hear the little tap-tap of her shoes coming along the passage. Then the door opened and shut. Mother saw her, so did I, and I would follow her all round the room with my eyes. Dad only saw the door open and shut, but he heard the soft click-click of her heels."

"Must have been nerve-racking for your father, I should think," observed Vance. "There's something beastly about a door working on its own," he added lamely, then in a more serious tone, "You know, I can't think why a ghost ever stays in a place where it was not happy when it wasn't a ghost. And you'd think that when it found all the old places changing, it would — er — bunk away as quick as it could."

"Yes, I've thought that, too," said Celia slowly, "but don't you think that if a person has an obsession — like she had — and then dies suddenly, that obsession remains and keeps them from going any further; and then, perhaps, to them the places they used to know look just the same always. You know, I'm really sorry for our little mauve lady. Wouldn't it be simply splendid if we could help her to remove the obsession and let her go on?"

"Yes, I suppose it would," said Vance getting up. "But how would one do it? By digging up the smuggler's treasures or empty barrels? No, that would be no good because she wouldn't know it." He got up. "Yes, it would be a fine thing to do, but damnably difficult."

"Damnably difficult," echoed Celia.

"Best two out of three?" said Vance suddenly.

"Right!" she answered. "Get the racquets."

That night Bobby Vance went to bed late and exhausted. He thought no more about the lady in lilac, until about two in the morning he distinctly heard a door open and shut, and then the click of high-heeled shoes coming down a passage. Now Vance was wide awake and sitting up. His door opened slowly, then shut. She was in the room. She walked over to his bed and stood looking at him.

Vance put out his hand to touch her. She looked so real in the half-light. She evaded him and walked to the window. She really walked, he could hear her heels on the oilcloth. Suddenly she put her hands to her face and began to cry.

Vance got out of bed and went to her. His sensations were peculiar, he felt overwhelmingly sorry for this poor wraith who seemed to be doomed to eternal disquietude. Even so, he had to *know*.

"Can I help you?" he called out. "Isn't there anything I can do?"

She took no notice, she even appeared not to hear. Slowly she moved to the door, opened it and went down the stairs.

He followed her into the garden and had almost caught up with her when she vanished.

Mechanically Vance bent down, picked up a stick and stuck it in the ground where she had disappeared, then went back to bed.

When he awoke next morning, he found that his mind was still filled with thoughts of her. "It would be a great thing to understand a ghost," he murmured the words as if there was someone listening, then "to understand that deep mystery which men have tried to fathom since the world began." Here was his chance, he knew it; a spirit in distress had come to him for help. If he could but give that help by so doing, he would discover the relationship between this world and the next. But how could he help unless she gave him some inkling of what it was that she wanted? He couldn't be expected to know everything, and as yet she hadn't given him a lead, had she? A lead? Was that it? Did she mean him to follow her? To follow her? But where to? Well, he had followed her, down the garden, down to the place where she had vanished after his first sighting. Was that the clue she offered? That was the very same spot where she had disappeared a second time. If that was a sign, what next? He could hardly follow where she went, into the earth.

Vance stiffened. But could he not follow? Perhaps, perhaps, that was it! He could dig. He could dig, and find…?

He cursed. Damn it all, what did it matter what he found. He would have a shot at it.

"Good heavens! There's the gong. Where did I put my shaving-soap?"

After breakfast he went round the outhouses, found a spade and fork. He began to dig; he dug all day, and he found nothing. He was disgusted and fed up when Berrie came along.

"My dear fellow!" he expostulated, "You mustn't do this sort of thing. You'll go off your head, you know, and you'll spoil my garden. You'll have to fill that hole up again, too, or you'll be having someone falling in and breaking his neck."

"I'm awfully sorry, Berrie," said Vance. "I am an ass. I'll come in now and fill this up tomorrow morning; no one will come by before then."

"All right! But stick a plank over it. There isn't one? Oh, well! Never mind, come on in."

Vance decided to go to bed early to sleep off his disappointment and his disgust with himself.

About half-eleven he woke up and recalled the conversation he had had with Celia the day before. It would be a great thing to help a ghost, and by helping to find out, Celia would think him very kind, Berrie would think him a clever fellow and, dash it all, Berrie would be right. If only there were some way of talking to a ghost! If only there were some way of knowing. He sat upright in bed. There it was again, a door opening and shutting and the click-click-click of high-heeled shoes...

She was there again, standing by the window crying. If only he could help her; if only he could talk to her, if only he could understand her.

Vance sprang out of bed.

"Can't I do anything for you? Oh, do let me help you!" he implored.

She turned to him, gave him one sorrowful look and went to the door. Again he followed her to the garden. Yes, she was going to the same place as before, he would follow her. He would follow her, even to... He *was* following her — then he slipped, and as he fell, he remembered.

JOE BERRIE and the Rev John Weymouth were sitting together on the little veranda in front of Merley Rectory.

Berrie had been talking, but now as he mused, he flicked his cigarette ash among the brilliant flowers of a red geranium which stood in a pot near his chair.

The Rev John Weymouth waited for more, but Berrie went on flicking his cigarette ash. At last the old rector spoke himself. "So next day you found him dead in the hole he had dug the day before," he observed.

"Yes," said Berrie shortly. He paused then went on suddenly, "You know, what beats me is how an athletic chap like Vance could manage to break his neck in a rotten little hole like that."

"A very sad story," remarked the rector.

"Yes," said Berrie, "and you know, Weymouth, it's a dashed funny thing but now," and unconsciously he lowered his voice, "now there's two of 'em." He met the rector's incredulous stare with steady eyes. "Oh! I know I can't see 'em, but by Jupiter I *can* hear them and Celia, poor girl, she went back to London after the second night," he paused again. "She liked Vance, you know."

"Ah!" said the old man, "It's ill work meddling with spirits. Even so they which dwell upon the earth may understand nothing but that which is upon the earth and He that dwelleth above the Heavens may only understand the things which are above the height of the Heavens," he quoted softly.

Berrie got up suddenly and giving the geranium a sudden and vicious kick, strolled slowly into the house.

THE CURIOUS AFFAIR IN NUT ROW

Always take notice of a woman," Divisional Detective Chief Inspector Luke spoke the words, casting a shameless glance at the pretty girl who had come in with Mr Campion. That evening he was in tremendous, not to say outrageous, form as he sat there on the narrow table in the upstairs private bar of the Platelayer's Arms looking like some magnificent black tom-cat in his tight sharp clothes.

It was one of those raw spring nights when the noise of the traffic sounds unnaturally close and there is a warning blast of freezing air whenever the outside door is opened. The rush-hour was at its height and it was as yet a little too early to go home, undoubtedly the right time for story-telling.

"It was listening to a woman who could hardly speak, bless her, save to say 'yeth,' which got me my first real promotion." As he spoke slowly Luke crossed his eyes, blew out his cheeks into dumplings and favoured us with a simper that was both innocent and arch, so that his voluble young woman appeared before us. "She worked in a tobacconist just behind the old St Mary's Road Police Station. We called her Mossy and she looked it — soft, you know, and green — she lived only for the movies and thought I ought to be a film star. I used to go round and talk to her when old George Misery Bull, the CID sergeant there in those days, got both of us crying with the dreariness of life."

Luke gave us a fleeting glimpse of a sad, fat man with a forehead like a bloodhound's and, with a fluid hand, he sketched for us a large and pendulous stomach.

Luke went on cheerfully. "It was a long winter that year and that brought out the lunatics. The cold does, you know. At the end of September they start getting a grievance, by Guy Fawkes' Night they start writing to *The Times*, after Christmas they're coming to the police. I'm not kidding. You want to watch out if you feel it coming on. Our particular headache that winter was Burberry Square. You know it?"

Mr Campion's knowledge of London was phenomenal. "The Society of Marine Research," he murmured immediately.

"That's the place." Luke shot him a swift, respectful glance. "On the north side; great tall houses, all dust, stairs and appalling improvements. George called it Nut Row. It wasn't residential except for one or two hide-outs in the attics." Luke bent his head smartly sideways as if to avoid an imaginary sloping ceiling and so vivid was his pantomime that several of his listeners bent their heads with him.

"At the time I'm talking about there was only one old fellow actually living in the entire block. He was up under the roof in the house next door to the Society of Marine Whatnot. Quite a snug little place he had there but it was a fine old houseful; on the floor below were the offices of a vegetarian magazine; under them a postage-stamp exchange and on the ground floor and in the basement a gaggle of old ladies sorted bundles for the Solomon Islanders every afternoon except Saturdays. Next door this Marine outfit had the whole building; they held meetings, gave lectures, and conducted a private war with their rivals over in Victoria, the Guild of Aquatic Science."

Luke glanced round his audience, his brows two circumflex

accents. "They were all a bit funny," he said seriously. "Even the Society, which is really quite well-known and just the ticket, seemed to be going over the edge. They'd got hold of a prehistoric fish which had landed them with a lot of publicity. It was older than the coelacanth — that's the one without the lungs, isn't it? Well, this one hadn't got a stomach either. Just solid fish all the way through or something of the sort." He was not exactly depicting the unfortunate beast, but a fleeting expression of acute introspection did suggest the unhappy brute.

"It was alive, too," he continued, the words pouring out of him as always they did when he was excited. "I saw it myself. Some Chinaman had got hold of it while he was doing his laundry in some sort of river they've got out there. It had been flown back at great expense and the Society was trying to keep it alive in a specially heated and suitably polluted tank. They didn't exactly put it on show, but they'd let you have a dekko if you were interested and ready to subscribe.

"I knew about it because Sir Bernard Walfish, who was the President of the Society, had a row with Sir Thingummy Something who was the head of the Guild at Victoria. Sir Thingummy wanted to dissect the thing in the cause of science, and it came to raised eyebrows on both sides. I was sent down to explain to Sir Bernard why the Metropolitan Police didn't feel his pet needed a police guard, unless he felt like paying for one. That's how I knew about the place and why the address wasn't new to me when we had complaints from Mr Theodore Hooky, the old boy in the roof next door."

"The man who lived over the vegetarian magazine," Mr Campion explained for those who were not paying full attention.

"That's right. In fact, we didn't know he was there at all until he telephoned one morning and, when we listened to him, we thought he couldn't be *all* there. Then, just about lunchtime, he called in at the station and we knew damned well he wasn't."

Luke paused, glanced sharply behind him, and came back to

his audience wearing an expression in which belligerence and suspicion were blended horrifically.

"He complained of saucerites."

"Oh dear," protested Mr Campion. "*Not flying* saucerites!"

"No error!" Luke's grimace confirmed Mr Campion's diagnosis. "He seemed to us to have it badly. We started off by thinking what a nice old boy he was, so polite, so sensitive, so sensible. Then, just when he had us eating out of his hand, an extraordinary expression came over his face and out it all came. Men from Mars. He didn't mind them himself, he said, but he couldn't think they'd do the country much good. The alarming thing was that he made it all sound so very factual. According to him, sometimes they made a mass descent on the roofs, sometimes they just sat on the stairs outside his flat and wouldn't move, and sometimes he only heard them making a wet sort of whistling which he took to be their way of trying to talk. They had globular eyes, he said, scaly skin and great splay feet like ducks. And, as he talked, all the time he had this insane look on his face."

"Poor fellow!" Mr Campion spoke with feeling.

"Weren't we all!" Luke was unmoved. "We had troubles enough of our own, and after we'd heard his tale for the third time then he began to telephone us in the small hours. The novelty had worn off and we began to think we'd have to pull him in, and that meant doctors and committal proceedings and almost certainly angry relatives." Luke shook his dark head. "We made the usual discreet inquiries and the more we learned about Mr Theodore Hooky the stickier it all looked. He was a bit of a recluse, but he was in all the reference-books with lots of letters after his name and he belonged to several of the fancier clubs. We waited but there were no complaints from anyone else and Mr Hooky kept his troubles just for us. We didn't go round to his place but each time he talked to us we fobbed him off with promises. It was all we could do and after the first few days we sort of got used to him. He became just one of those things."

Luke sighed: "And then, one day I went to Mossy's for some cigarettes and ran into him coming out. It was the first time I had ever seen him in the street. I said, 'Good evening.' He stared, eyed my feet in his crazy way, and shot past, leaving me somehow uncomfortable."

He glanced down at his huge black shoes and grinned. "Quack, quack," he said. "That's all I was thinking when Mossy started up. I didn't listen to her at first but after a bit I heard her say: 'He was the surgeon and she didn't half look lovely. You could see his hands shake. It was in colour and they were both green. Sinister it was.'"

Luke gave a remarkable imitation of a soft, thick London voice trembling with remembered thrills and there was in his bright eyes an innocent glee which was infectious.

"That caught me," he said. "I don't know why, and I said, 'Who was?' 'Why, he was,' she said. 'That man who's just gone out. He's an actor.' I said. 'Get away!'" but she stuck to it. She said she had seen him at the cinema and his name was Martin Treower and he played bit-parts. 'He's always the one who's all strung-up,' she said. 'He's in my annual; I'll show you.' And she did too."

Luke's eyes widened. "It took a bit of time, but she got down under the counter and came out with some film annual, and we went through it together. I didn't believe her, you know, but she found what she was looking for, a half-page illustrated article. I couldn't believe my eyes but there was no getting away from it. There it was, 'Martin Treower: The Man with the Lunatic Face.' It seems he was a character-actor specialising in neurotic parts, and they showed a line of thumbnail portraits of him, each of them showing him in a different costume, but all with the same unforgettable crazy expression. He was the Mad Surgeon, the Insane Butler, the Demented Executioner. He'd made a study of it. The moment he put on that expression even the least intelligent member of any audience knew he was round the bend and that nothing he said could be relied on."

Luke began to laugh. "I was standing there gaping when Mossy lit a squib under me. 'He's just finished a part, I expect, because he came in for a copy of the paper all those actors take when they're out of work.' Blow me down! I didn't stop running!"

He rubbed his long hands together and the vigour of the gesture brought the bustle of that long-ago evening into the private bar of the Platelayer's Arms.

"We got 'em all right," said Luke, "but it was touch and go because I couldn't get George to believe me. He thought we ought to go round to the attic flat first to contact the real Theodore Hooky, but that would have been fatal. There simply wasn't time. George gave way at last and we did the thing properly. We posted three men outside the building and my mate and I went into the Society's house and just waited. At two in the morning they came up the fire-escape — four of them — right into our arms."

"What on earth are you talking about?" The pretty girl who had been watching Luke's excitement with growing bewilderment spoke involuntarily. "Who came up the fire-escape? Where? What for?"

Luke beamed at her. "My dear, you have forgotten the Father of All Fish," he said happily. "The Guild wanted it, remember? The Society wouldn't part with it. So, strictly in the cause of science, of course, as they explained later to the magistrate, a party of interested young gentlemen decided to nip in and take it for themselves. They made the most elaborate preparations. Had to. The tank was twelve feet deep. So two of them wore kit suitable for the operation. By the time we got hold of them they did indeed look like Men from Mars. They'd decided to go through the roof because the doors were too public, the locks too good and the windows barred. It was as simple as that."

Mr Campion took off his spectacles and his light eyes were dancing with interest.

"How very ingenious of them to employ that actor to prepare the ground," he said. "Mr Hooky was the one and only witness who was almost certain to see them on the roof. It would have been his natural instinct to call the police."

"And the police would have given him a rocket," put in Luke with relish, "a rocket of which the police would never have heard the last. We'd have been fooled, just because our simple minds had been prepared for just that sort of call at just that sort of time from the Man with the Lunatic Face." A smile narrowed his wide mouth and he glanced at the girl. "No one in the Met felt like advertising that bit, that's why Mr Martin Treower was never prosecuted. We just re-christened him and hid him in the files."

"Re-christened him?" The girl took the cue he offered, and Luke's eyelids drooped. "Maybe it's because we're Londoners," he quoted contentedly, "but he's there all right under Treower, Martin, actor. The man with the cuckoo clock!"

WHAT TO DO WITH AN AGEING
DETECTIVE

I came out of my interview with Mr Albert Campion feeling
rather sad. He had been so nice. As we parted, he took my
hand.

"My dear girl," he said, looking at me with that kindly wryness
which no longer wrung my heart. "How *can* I?"

"Can you what?" I was abrupt with him.

"Well…" He was still modest, still shy, still a trifle vague, not to
say incoherent for a modern world. "Hop about. Pull guns and
shoot lines. Pretend I like the police… I mean, everybody knows
how old I am. *You* saw to that, fixing it as the same age as the
century so we shouldn't get muddled. I'm not complaining, dearest. I only point out that by the time the next tale comes out I'll
be…" he blushed faintly, "well, sixtyish."

"Yes," I murmured, colouring faintly myself. "Yes, I see. Don't
you like the police anymore?"

"Not awfully." The pale eyes betrayed a blue severity I had not
noticed long ago. "They're all right. Good chaps doing their job I
suppose but it's a tatty old job, sweetie. Don't you think so?"

"No." I said hastily, kissing him firmly and pushing him back
inside his flat door in Bottle Street. "No, I don't. If I did, we'd

neither of us be here. Bless you, see you soon. You get set in your armchair."

With which injunction I came away and was wandering along the damp pavements wondering why it was that the four years difference in our ages should make such an appalling difference to our outlooks and if it was to be my turn next, when the little accident happened.

I had taken a short cut through a mews and as I passed below one of the tiny flats above the garages which lined the path, an upper window opened and someone shaking a large traveling rug out of it, dropped it neatly over my head. He came thundering down to extricate me and as I fought my way out of the folds, I saw to my astonishment an old friend who I had thought must be dead by this time. Magersfontein Lugg, vast, white and walrus-moustached loomed before me.

"'Ullo, duck," he said. "Come to supper? There's a tin of 'errings on the table only opened this morning." He led the way up a rickety wooden staircase to a largish room which had been converted only too obviously from the stable loft it once had been. Its only furniture was three huge Victorian wardrobes set round the walls and in the centre a kitchen table and one wooden chair. On the table there was the inevitable tin and also a fine array of cleaning materials, clothes brushes and so on, all the paraphernalia of the valet's trade. I kept looking at Lugg in aston-ishment and he met my gaze, unwinking.

Finally I could bear it no longer.

"Magers," I said brutally. "I don't want to hurt your feelings but by my calculation, and my goodness I ought to know, you must be about one hundred and two. What do you think you're doing?"

He regarded me with hurt astonishment as if a fond mother yak had suddenly slapped her youngster for no reason.

"Doin'?" he said. "Goin' about my business same like you ought to be. I'm a man's gent an' I'm gent-ing. See this 'ere 'orse rug? It's one of two wot was woven special for 'is Majesty King

Edward the Seventh and 'is good Lady. Gord-bless them both! They 'ad one and this 'ere's the other. Nice, ain't it? 'Arf inch thick."

"Lugg!" I said aghast. "You haven't left Albert — not without telling me?"

"Left the ole guv'nor!" Great drops of sentiment glistened on the bald forehead. "Nah! I wouldn't leave the ole dear for a fortune. I'm on loan."

I looked about me nervously. The large mahogany doors, tight closed, seemed suddenly sinister. "Who — who to? No time machines, Magers! No monkey tricks with the century."

"Not on your Nellie!" He was scandalised. "Not me. This is 1958 oll right. No I'm just doin' a bit for young Chris. 'E come into this 'ere clobber — left 'im by the valet of 'is great-uncle Edwin — and I'm 'elpin 'im to look after it." He flicked open one of the glowing mahogany doors and my glance rested on a dark line of shrouded coats, each in its Holland cover. Below them was a line of narrow leather toes, opulent in the light; chestnut, tan, ebony, ash.

He closed the door with a sigh. "They fit Chris, see?" he said. "Old Cherrystone 'oo 'ad 'ad 'em left to 'im by Sir Edwin, watched over young Chris from the day 'e was born 'oping 'e'd grow the right size. Very tall Sir Edwin was. Tall and narrer wiv one shoulder 'igher than the other."

"Oh dear!" I said involuntarily. "What a pity. Everything has to be altered I suppose?"

"No. I show 'im 'ow to 'old 'isself."

"I see." I was aware of a sneaking sympathy for the young man, whoever he was. "What is the rest of his name?"

Lugg glanced about him with the conspiratorial air I knew so well. "Do you remember that bruvver of the ole guvnor's?"

"Of Albert Campion's?" I found I was lowering my voice also.

He nodded. "The one 'oo was dropped on 'is 'ead at Eton. Chris is 'is youngest. 'E's a nice lad. Got no money. Works 'ard as a

PRO. Very fashionable, quite up to date. Stick around. It might be worth your while, I'll make something of 'im, I shouldn't wonder."

"I think you might," I muttered. I was bewildered. "Lugg, who *are* you? I mean if Albert has got older, why haven't you?"

He took up a slender shoe the colour of a conker and began to bone it. He was a trifle amused I thought.

"Wot a question to arsk!" he said presently. "You should keep up with the times. Us in the Know is all readin' the Greeks these days. You should 'ave a basin full yourself when the washin's done. You was sweet on Albert in the ole days. 'E was an ideal of yours like, wasn't 'e?" He leered at me. "I wasn't, was I?"

"Hardly!" He was insufferable and I thought once again as I have a thousand times up and down the years, what a cracking old horror he is. To my dismay I started to tell him so.

"You're such an impossible snob!" I burst out. "You're a figure of fun and fantasy, only interested in junk and cleaning up and…"

"Eggsactly!" He stood there nodding at me his eyes gleaming with fearful knowingness. "Eggsactly. Some think I'm not quite the article and some think the considerable difference between me and St Anfony's Pig is precisely the difference between you and Flaubert. Is there anything else you'd like to say whilst you're about it?"

"No. No of course not," I muttered hastily, anxious not to offend him. "I was only wondering when you were going to get round to being your age."

An expression of great spitefulness spread over his moon face.

"W'en you do, my lady," he said. "Jest eggsactly w'en *you* do. Put that in your pipe and smoke it. Now, do you want to be introduced to young Chris or don't you?

"I sharnt asrk you twice. 'E'll be along any minute now. What about it?"

What could I do?

ABOUT THE AUTHOR

Margery Allingham, born in 1904 to Emily and Herbert Allingham, was an esteemed English novelist, author, and editor of *Christian Globe* and the *New London Journal*. Considered one of the four "Queens of Crime" from the golden age of detective fiction, Allingham began writing stories and plays at a young age and published her first novel, *Blackkerchief Dick*, at nineteen. She later studied drama and speech training at Regent Street Polytechnic in London. Allingham is best known for her character Albert Campion, a sleuth first introduced in *The Crime of Black Dudley*. Campion was featured in seventeen subsequent novels, and even more short stories Allingham continued to write until her death on June 30, 1966.

THE ALBERT CAMPION MYSTERIES

FROM OPEN ROAD MEDIA

INTEGRATED MEDIA

Find a full list of our authors and titles at www.openroadmedia.com

FOLLOW US
@OpenRoadMedia